MISSING

Look out for more titles
in the MISSING series

**When Lightning Strikes
Code Name Cassandra
Sanctuary**

MISSING
Safe House

Meg Cabot
Writing as Jenny Carroll

SIMON AND SCHUSTER

SIMON AND SCHUSTER

First published in Great Britain in 2003 by Pocket Books,
an imprint of Simon & Schuster UK Ltd.
Africa House, 64-78 Kingsway, London WC2B 6AH

This edition published in 2004 by Simon & Schuster UK Ltd.
A CBS COMPANY

Originally published in the USA in 2002 by Pocket Pulse,
an imprint of Simon & Schuster Inc., New York.

A CIP catalogue record for this book is available
from the British Library upon request.

ISBN-10: 0-6898-6093-5
ISBN-13: 978-0-6898-6093-5

5 7 9 10 8 6

Printed by Cox & Wyman Ltd, Reading, Berkshire

With many thanks to Jen Brown, John Henry Dreyfuss, David Walton, and especially Benjamin Egnatz.

CHAPTER

1

I didn't know about the dead girl until the first day of school.

It wasn't my fault. I swear it wasn't. I mean, how was I supposed to have known? It wasn't like I'd been home. If I'd been home, of course I would have seen it in the paper, or on the news, or whatever. I would have heard people talking about it.

But I hadn't been home. I'd been stuck four hours north of home, at the Michigan dunes, in my best friend Ruth Abramowitz's summerhouse. The Abramowitzes go to the dunes for the last two weeks of August every summer, and this year, they invited me to go along.

I wasn't going to go at first. I mean, who'd want to spend two weeks trapped in a summerhouse with Ruth's twin brother Skip? Um, not me. Skip still chews with his mouth open even

1

though he is sixteen and should know better. Plus he is like Grand Dragon Master of our town's Dungeons & Dragons population, in spite of the Trans Am he bought with his bar mitzvah money.

On top of which, Mr. Abramowitz has this thing about cable, and the only telephone he'll allow in his vacation house is his cell, which is reserved for emergency use only, like if one of his clients gets thrown in the clink or whatever. (He's a lawyer.)

So you can see, of course, why I was like, "Thanks, but no thanks," to Ruth's invitation.

But then my parents said that they were spending the last two weeks of August driving my brother Mike and all his stuff up to Harvard, where he was going to be starting his freshman year, and that Great-aunt Rose would be coming to stay with me and my other brother, Douglas, while they were gone.

Never mind that I am sixteen and Douglas is twenty and that we do not need parental supervision, particularly in the form of a seventy-five-year-old lady who is obsessed with solitaire and my sex life (not that I have one). Great-aunt Rose was coming to stay, and I was informed that I could like it or lump it.

I chose neither. Instead of coming home after my stint as a camp counselor at the Lake Wawasee Camp for Gifted Child Musicians, which was how I got to spend my summer vacation, I went with the Abramowitzes to the dunes.

Hey. Even watching Skip eat grilled peanut-butter-and-banana sandwiches morning, noon, and night for two weeks beat spending five minutes with Great-aunt Rose, who likes to talk about how in her day, only cheap girls wore dungarees.

Seriously. Dungarees. That's what she calls them.

You can see why I chose the dunes instead.

And truthfully, the two weeks didn't go so badly.

Oh, don't get me wrong. I didn't have a good time or anything. How could I? Because while we'd been slaving away at Camp Wawasee, Ruth had been working very hard on her teen social development, and she'd managed to acquire a boyfriend.

That's right. An actual boyfriend, whose parents—wouldn't you know it—also had a house on the dunes, like ten minutes away from Ruth's.

I tried to be supportive, because Scott was Ruth's first real boyfriend—you know, the first guy she'd liked who actually liked her back, and who didn't seem to mind being seen holding her hand in public, and all of that.

But let's face it, when someone invites you to stay with them for two weeks, and then spends those two weeks basically hanging out with somebody else, it can be a little disappointing. I spent the majority of my daylight hours lying on the beach, reading used paperbacks, and most of my nights trying to beat Skip at Crash Bandicoot on his Sony Playstation.

Oh, yeah. It was a real thrill, my summer vacation.

The good part, Ruth kept pointing out to me, was that by being at the dunes, I was not at my house waiting for my boyfriend—or whatever he is—to call. This, Ruth informed me, was an important part of the courtship ritual . . . you know, the not-being-there-when-he-calls part. Because then, Ruth explained, he'll wonder where you are, and start making up these scenarios in his head about where you could be. Maybe he'll even think you're with another guy!

Somehow, this is supposed to make him like you more.

Which is all good, I guess, but is sort of contingent on one thing:

The guy actually has to call.

See, if he doesn't call, he can't discover that you aren't home. My boyfriend—or should I say, the guy I like, since he is not technically my boyfriend, as we have never been out on an actual date—never calls. This is because he is of the opinion that I am what is commonly referred to in the great state of Indiana as jailbait.

And he's already on probation.

Don't ask me what for. Rob won't tell me.

That's his name. Rob Wilkins. Or the Jerk, as Ruth refers to him.

But I don't think it's fair to call him the Jerk, because it isn't as if he ever led me on. I mean, he made it pretty much clear from the moment he found out I was sixteen that there could never be anything between us. At least, not for a couple more years.

And really, you know, I am fine with that. I mean, there are lots of fish in the sea.

And okay, maybe they don't all have eyes the color of fog as it rolls in over the lake just before sunrise, or a set of washboard abs, or a completely cherried-out Indian motorcycle they've rebuilt from scratch in their barn.

But, you know, they're male. Ostensibly.

Whatever. The point is, I was gone for two weeks: no phone, no TV, no radio, no media resources whatsoever. It was a vacation, all right? A real vacation. Well, except for the having fun part.

So how was I supposed to know that while I was gone, a girl in my class had croaked? No one mentioned a word about it to me.

Not until homeroom, anyway.

That's the problem, really, with living in such a small town. I've been in the same homeroom with the same people since middle school. Oh, sure, occasionally somebody will move out of town, or a new kid will show up. But for the most part, it's the same old faces, year after year.

Which was why, the first day of my junior year at Ernest Pyle High School, I slid into the second seat from the door in homeroom. I always ended up in the second seat from the door in homeroom. That's because, in homeroom, we sit alphabetically, and my last name—Mastriani— puts me second in the Ms for my class, behind

Amber Mackey. Amber Mackey always sits in front of me in homeroom. Always.

Except that day. That day, she didn't show up.

Hey, I didn't know why. How was I supposed to know? Amber had never not shown up for the first day of school before. She was no more of an intellectual dynamo than I am, but you never actually *do* anything the first day of school, so why not show up? Besides, unlike me, Amber had always liked school. She was a cheerleader. She was always all, "We've got spirit, yes, we do, we've got spirit, how 'bout *you?*"

You know the type.

A type like that, I don't know, you'd expect she'd show up the first day of school, just in order to show off her tan.

So I left the first chair in the row of seats by the door empty. Everyone filed in, looking carefully nonchalant, even though you knew most of them—the girls, anyway—had spent hours putting together exactly the right outfit to show off how much weight they'd lost over their summer . . . or their new highlights . . . or their chemically whitened teeth.

Everyone sat down where they were supposed to—we'd done this enough times to know by the eleventh grade who sat behind whom in homeroom—and people were all, "Hey, how was your summer?" or "Oh, my God, you're so tan," or "That skirt is so *cute!*"

And then the bell rang, and Mr. Cheaver came in with the roster and told us all to settle down, even though at eight fifteen in the morning, nobody was exactly boisterous.

Then he looked down at the roster, hesitated, and said, "Mastriani."

I raised my hand, even though Mr. Cheaver was standing practically in front of me, and had had me last year for World Civ, so it wasn't as if he didn't recognize me. Granted, Ruth and I had spent a considerable amount of our Wawasee paychecks at the clothing outlet stores outside Michigan City, and I was wearing, at Ruth's insistence, an actual skirt to school, something that might have thrown Mr. C off a little, since I had never before shown up to school in anything besides jeans and a T-shirt.

Still, as Ruth pointed out, I was never going to get Rob to realize how much he had erred in not going out with me unless I got someone else to take me out (and was seen by Rob in this other person's company), so, according to Ruth, I had to "make an effort" this year. I was in Esprit from head to toe, but it wasn't as much that I was hoping to attract potential suitors as it was that, having gotten back as late as I had the night before (Ruth absolutely refuses to exceed the speed limit when she drives, even when there is not a culvert in sight in which a highway patrolman could be hiding), I had no other clean clothes.

Maybe, I thought, Mr. Cheaver doesn't recognize me in my miniskirt and cotton sweater set. So I went, "Here, Mr. C," to show him I was present.

"I can see you, Mastriani," Mr. C said, in his usual lazy drawl. "Move up one."

I looked at the empty seat in front of me.

"Oh, no, Mr. C," I said. "That's Amber's seat. She must be late or something. But she'll be here."

There was a strange silence. Really. I mean, not all silences are the same, even though you would think by definition—the absence of sound—they would be.

This one, however, was *more* silent than most silences. Like everyone, all at once, had suddenly decided to hold their breath.

Mr. Cheaver—who was also holding his breath—narrowed his eyes at me. There weren't many teachers at Ernie Pyle High whom I could stand, but Mr. C was one of them. That's because he didn't play favorites. He hated every single one of us just about equally. He maybe hated me a little less than some of my peers, because last year, I had actually done the homework he'd assigned, as I'd found World Civ quite interesting, especially the parts about the wholesale slaughter of entire populations.

"Where have you been, Mastriani?" Mr. Cheaver wanted to know. "Amber Mackey's not coming back this year."

Seriously, how was I to have known?

"Oh, really?" I said. "Did her parents move or something?"

Mr. C just looked at me in a very displeased manner, while the rest of the class suddenly exhaled, all at once, and started buzzing instead. I had no idea what they were talking about, but from the scandalized looks on their faces, I could tell I had really put my foot in it this time. Tisha Murray and Heather Montrose looked particularly contemptuous of me. I thought about getting up and cracking their heads together, but I've tried that before, and it doesn't actually work.

But another thing I was trying to "make an effort" to do my junior year—besides cause some innocent young man to fall completely in love with me so I could stroll, ever so casually, hand-in-hand with him in front of the garage where Rob had been working since he graduated last year—was not get into fistfights. Seriously. I had spent enough weeks in detention back in tenth grade thanks to my inability to control my rage impulse. I was not going to make the same mistake this year.

That was one of the other reasons—besides my total lack of clean Levis—that I'd gone for the miniskirt. It wasn't so easy to knee somebody in the groin while clad in a Lycra/rayon blend.

Maybe, I thought, as I observed the expressions of the people around me, Amber had gotten herself knocked up, and everyone knew it but me. Hey, in spite of Coach Albright's Health class, mandatory for all sophomores, in which we were warned of the perils of unsafe sex, it happens. Even to cheerleaders.

But apparently not to Amber Mackey, since Mr. C looked down at me and went, tonelessly, "Mastriani. She's dead."

"Dead?" I echoed. "Amber Mackey?" Then, like an idiot: "Are you sure?"

I don't know why I asked him that. I mean, if a teacher says somebody is dead, you can pretty much count on the fact that he's telling the truth. I'd just been so surprised. It probably sounds like a cliché, but Amber Mackey had always been . . . well, full of life. She hadn't been one of those cheerleaders you could hate. She'd never been purposefully mean to anyone, and she'd always had to try really hard to keep up with the other girls on the squad, both socially as well as athletically. Academically, she'd been no National Merit Scholar, either, if you get my drift.

But she'd tried. She'd always really tried.

Mr. C wasn't the one who answered me. Heather Montrose was.

"Yeah, she's dead," she said, her carefully glossed upper lip raised in disgust. "Where have you been, anyway?"

"Really," Tisha Murray said. "I'd have thought *Lightning Girl* would have had a clue, at least."

"What's the matter?" Heather asked me. "Your psychic radar on the fritz or something?"

I am not precisely what you would call popular, but since I do not make a habit of going around being a total bitch to people, like Heather and Tisha, there are folk who actually will come to my defense against them. One of them, Todd Mintz—linebacker on the varsity football team who was sitting behind me—went, "Jesus, would you two cool it? She doesn't do the psychic thing anymore. Remember?"

"Yeah," Heather said, with a flick of her long, blonde mane. "I heard."

"And I heard," Tisha said, "that just two weeks ago, she found some kid who'd been lost in a cave or something."

This was patently untrue. It had been a month ago. But I wasn't about to admit as much to the likes of Tisha.

Fortunately, I was spared from having to make any reply whatsoever by the tactful intervention of Mr. Cheaver.

"Excuse me," Mr. C said. "But while this may come as a surprise to some of you, I have a class to conduct here. Would you mind saving the personal chat until after the bell rings? Mastriani. Move up one."

I moved up one seat, as did the rest of our row. As we did so, I whispered to Todd, "So what happened to her, anyway?" thinking Amber had gotten leukemia or something, and that the cheerleaders would probably start having car washes all the time in order to raise money to help fight cancer. The Amber Fund, they'd probably call it.

But Amber's death had not been from natural causes, apparently. Not if what Todd whispered back was the truth.

"They found her yesterday," he said. "Facedown in one of the quarries. Strangled to death."

Oh.

CHAPTER

2

Now, who would do that?

Seriously. I want to know.

Who would strangle a cheerleader, and dump her body at the bottom of a limestone quarry?

I can certainly understand *wanting* to strangle a cheerleader. Our school harbors some of the meanest cheerleaders in North America. Seriously. It's like you have to pass a test proving you have no human compassion whatsoever just to get on the squad. The cheerleaders at Ernest Pyle High would sooner pluck out their own eyelashes than deign to speak to a kid who wasn't of their social caliber.

But actually to go through with it? You know, off one of them? It hardly seemed worth the effort.

And anyway, Amber hadn't been like the others. I had actually seen Amber smile at a Grit—

the derogatory name for the kids who were bused in from the rural routes to Ernie Pyle, the only high school in the county; kids who did not live on a rural route are referred to, imaginatively, as Townies.

Amber had been a Townie, like Ruth and me. But I had never observed her lording this fact over anyone, as I often had Heather and Tisha and their ilk. Amber, when selected as a team captain in PE, had never chosen all Townies first, then moved on to Grits. Amber, when walking down the hall with her books and pompons, had never sneered at the Grits' Wranglers and Lee jeans, the only "dungarees" they could afford. I had never seen Amber administer a "Grit test": holding up a pen and asking an unsuspecting victim what she had in her hand. (If the reply was "A pen," you were safe. If, however, you said, "A pin," you were labeled a Grit and laughed at for your Southern drawl.)

Is it any wonder that I have anger-management issues? I mean, seriously. Wouldn't you, if you had to put up with this crap on a daily basis?

Anyway, it just seemed to me a shame that, out of all the cheerleaders, Amber had been the one who'd had to die. I mean, I had actually liked her.

And I wasn't the only one, as I soon found out.

"Good job," somebody hissed as they passed me in the hallway while I walked to my locker.

"Way to go," somebody else said as I was coming out of Bio.

And that wasn't all. I got a sarcastic "Thanks a lot, *Lightning Girl*," by the drinking fountains and was called a "skank" as I went by a pack of Pompettes, the freshmen cheerleaders.

"I don't get it," I said to Ruth in fourth period Orchestra as we were unpacking our instruments. "It's like people are blaming me or something for what happened to Amber. Like I had something to do with it."

Ruth, applying rosin to her cello bow, shook her head.

"That's not it," she said. She had gotten the scoop, apparently, in Honors English. "I guess when Amber didn't come home Friday night, her parents called the cops and stuff, but they didn't have any luck finding her. So I guess a bunch of people called your house, you know, thinking you might be able to track her down. You know. Psychically. But you weren't home, of course, and your aunt wouldn't give any of them my dad's emergency cell number, and there's no other way to reach us up at our summer place, so . . ."

So? So it *was* my fault. Or at the very least, Great-aunt Rose's fault. Now I had yet another reason to resent her.

Never mind that I have taken great pains to impress upon everyone the fact that I no longer have the psychic ability to find missing people. That thing last spring, when I'd been struck by lightning and could suddenly tell, just by looking at a photo of someone, where that someone was, had been a total fluke. I'd told that to the press, too. I'd told it to the cops, and to the FBI. Lightning Girl—which was how I'd been referred to by the media for a while there—no longer existed. My ESP had faded as mysteriously as it had arrived.

Except of course it hadn't really. I'd been lying to get the press—and the cops—off my back.

And, apparently, everyone at Ernest Pyle High School knew it.

"Look," Ruth said as she practiced a few chords. "It's not your fault. If anything, it's your whacked-out aunt's fault. She should have known it was an emergency and given them my dad's cell number. But even so, you know Amber. She wasn't the shiniest rock in the garden. She'd have gone out with Freddy Krueger if he'd asked her. It really isn't any wonder she ended up face-down in Pike's Quarry."

If this was meant to comfort me, it did not. I slunk back to the flute section, but I could not concentrate on what Mr. Vine, our Orchestra teacher, was saying to us. All I could think about was how at last year's talent show, Amber and her longtime boyfriend—Mark Leskowski, the Ernie Pyle High Cougars quarterback—had done this very lame rendition of *Anything You Can Do I Can Do Better*, and how serious Amber had been about it, and how certain she'd been that she and Mark were going to win.

They didn't, of course—first prize went to a guy whose Chihuahua howled every time it heard the theme song to *Seventh Heaven*—but Amber had been thrilled by winning second place.

Thrilled, I couldn't help thinking, to death.

"All right," Mr. Vine said just before the bell rang. "For the rest of the week, we'll hold chair auditions. Horns tomorrow, strings on Wednesday, winds on Thursday, and percussion on Friday. So do me a favor and practice for a change, will you?"

The bell for lunch rang. Instead of tearing out of there, though, most people reached beneath their seats and pulled out sandwiches and cans of warm soda. That's because the vast majority of kids in Symphonic Orchestra are geeks, afraid of venturing into the caf, where they might be ridiculed by their more athletically endowed peers. Instead, they spend their lunch hour in the music wing, munching soggy tuna fish sandwiches and arguing about who makes a better starship captain, Kirk or Picard.

Not Ruth and me, though. In the first place, I have never been able to stand the thought of eating in a room in which the words "spit valve" are mentioned so often. In the second place, Ruth had already explained that what with our new wardrobes—and her recent weight loss—we were not going to hide in the bowels of the music wing. No, we were going to see and be seen. Though Ruth's heart still belonged to Scott, the fact was, he lived three hundred miles away. We had only ten more months to secure a prom date, and Ruth insisted we start immediately.

Before we got out of the orchestra room, however, we were accosted by one of my least favorite people, fellow flutist Karen Sue Hankey, who made haste to inform me that I could give up all hope of hanging onto third chair this year, as she had been practicing for four hours a day and taking private lessons from a music professor at a nearby college.

"Great," I said, as Ruth and I tried to slip past her.

"Oh, and by the way," Karen Sue added, "that was real nice, how you were there for Amber and all."

But if I thought that'd be the worst I'd hear on the subject, I was sadly mistaken. It was ten times worse in the cafeteria. All I wanted to do was get my Tater Tots and go, but do you think they'd let me? Oh, no.

Because the minute we got in line, Heather Montrose and her evil clone Tisha slunk up behind us and started making remarks.

I don't get it. I really don't. I mean, the way I'd left things last spring, when school let out, was that I didn't have my psychic powers anymore. So how was everyone so sure I'd lied? I mean, the only person who knew any differently was Ruth, and she'd never tell.

But somebody had been doing some talking, that was for sure.

"So, what's it like?" Heather wanted to know as she sidled up behind us in the grill line. "I mean, knowing that somebody died because of you."

"Amber didn't die because of anything I did, Heather," I said, keeping my eyes on the tray I was sliding along past the bowls of sickly looking lime Jell-O and suspiciously lumpy tapioca pudding. "Amber died because somebody killed her. Somebody who was not me."

"Yeah," Tisha agreed. "But, according to the coroner, she was held against her will for a while before she was killed. They were lickator marks on her."

"Ligature," Ruth corrected her.

"Whatever," Tisha said. "That means if you'd been around, you could have found her."

"Well, I wasn't around," I said. "Okay? Excuse me for going on vacation."

"Really, Tish," Heather said in a chiding voice. "She's got to go on vacation sometime. I mean, she probably needs it, living with that retard and all."

"Oh, God," I heard Ruth moan. Then she carefully lifted her tray out of the line of fire.

That's because, of course, Ruth knew. There aren't many things that will make me forget all the anger-management counseling I've received from Mr. Goodhart, upstairs in the guidance office. But even after nearly two years of being instructed to count to ten before giving in to my anger—and nearly two years of detention for having failed miserably in my efforts to do so— any derogatory mention of my brother Douglas still sets me off.

About a second after Heather made her ill-advised remark, she was pinned up against the cinder block wall behind her.

And my hand was what was holding her there. By her neck.

"Didn't anyone ever tell you," I hissed at her, my face about two inches from hers, "that it is rude to make fun of people who are less fortunate than you?"

Heather didn't reply. She couldn't, because I had hold of her larynx.

"Hey." A deep voice behind me sounded startled. "Hey. What's going on here?"

I recognized the voice, of course.

"Mind your own business, Jeff," I said. Jeff Day, football tackle and all around idiot, has also never been one of my favorite people.

"Let her go," Jeff said, and I felt one of his meaty paws land on my shoulder.

An elbow, thrust with precision, soon put an end to his intervention. As Jeff gasped for air behind me, I loosened my hold on Heather a little.

"Now," I said to her. "Are you going to apologize?"

But I had underestimated the amount of time it would take Jeff to recover from my blow. His sausage-like fingers again landed on my shoulder, and this time, he managed to spin me around to face him.

"You let her alone!" he bellowed, his face beet red from the neck up.

I think he would have hit me. I really do. And

at the time, I sort of relished the idea. Jeff would take a swing at me, I would duck, and then I'd go for his nose. I'd been longing to break Jeff Day's nose for some time. Ever since, in fact, the day he'd told Ruth she was so fat they were going to have to bury her in a piano case, like Elvis.

Only I didn't get a chance to break Jeff's nose that day. I didn't get a chance because someone strode up behind him just as he was drawing back his fist, caught it midswing, and wrapped his arm around his back.

"That how you guards get your kicks?" Todd Mintz demanded. "Beating up girls?"

"All right." A third and final voice, equally recognizable to me, broke the little party up. Mr. Goodhart, holding a tossed salad and a container of yogurt, nodded toward the cafeteria doors. "All of you. In my office. Now."

Jeff and Todd and I followed him resentfully. It wasn't until we were nearly at the door that Mr. Goodhart turned and called, with some exasperation, "You, too, Heather," that Heather came slinking along after us.

In Mr. Goodhart's office, we were informed that we were not "Starting the Year Off Right," and that we really ought to be "Setting a Better Example for the Younger Students," seeing as how we were all juniors now. It would "Behoove Us to Come Together and Try to Get Along," especially in the wake of the tragedy that had occurred over the weekend.

"I know Amber's death has shaken us all up,"

Mr. Goodhart said, sincerity oozing out of his every pore. "But let's try to remember that she would have wanted us to comfort one another in our grief, not get torn apart by petty bickering."

Out of all of us, Heather was the only one who'd never before been dragged into a counselor's office for fighting. So, of course, instead of keeping her mouth shut so we could all get out of there, she pointed a silk-wrapped fingernail at me and went, "She started it."

Todd and Jeff and I rolled our eyes. We knew what was coming next.

Mr. Goodhart launched into his "I Don't Care Who Started It, Fighting Is Wrong" speech. It lasted four and a half minutes, twenty seconds longer than last year's version. Then Mr. Goodhart went, "You're all good kids. You have unlimited potential, each of you. Don't throw it all away through violence against one another."

Then he said everyone could go.

Everyone except me, of course.

"It wasn't my fault," I said as soon as the others were gone. "Heather called Douglas a retard."

Mr. Goodhart shoveled a spoonful of yogurt into his mouth.

"Jess," he said, with his mouth full. "Is this how it's going to be again? You, in my office every day for fighting?"

"No," I said. I tugged on the hem of my miniskirt. Though I knew I looked good in it, I did feel just a tad naked. Also, it hadn't worked.

I'd gotten into a fight anyway. "I'm trying to do what you said. You know, the whole counting to ten thing. But it's just . . . everyone is going around, *blaming* me."

Mr. Goodhart looked puzzled. "Blaming you for what?"

"For what happened to Amber." I explained to him what everyone was saying.

"That's ridiculous," Mr. Goodhart said. "You couldn't have stopped what happened to Heather, even if you did still have your powers. Which you don't." He looked at me. "Do you?"

"Of course not," I said.

"So where are they getting the idea that you do?" Mr. Goodhart wondered.

"I don't know." I looked at the salad he was eating. "What happened to you?" I asked. "Where's the Quarter Pounder with cheese?" Ever since I'd met him, Mr. Goodhart's lunches had always consisted of a burger with a side of fries, usually super-sized.

He made a face. "I'm on a diet," he said. "Blood pressure and cholesterol are off the scale, according to my GP."

"Wow," I said. I knew how much he loved his fries. "Sorry."

"I'll live," he said with a shrug. "The question is, what are we going to do about you?"

What we decided to do about me was "Give Me Another Chance." "One More Strike," though, and "I Was Out."

Which meant detention. With a capital D.

We were chatting amiably about Mr. Goodhart's son, Russell, who'd just started crawling, when the secretary came in, looking worried.

"Paul," she said. "There are some men here from the sheriff's office. They want to pull Mark Leskowski out for questioning. You know, about the Mackey girl."

Mr. Goodhart looked concerned. "Oh, God," he said. "All right. Get Mark's parents on the phone, will you? And let Principal Feeney know."

I watched, fascinated, as the administrative staff of Ernie Pyle High went on red alert. The sudden burst of activity drove me from Mr. Goodhart's office, but I sank down onto a vinyl couch in the waiting room outside it, where I could observe uninterrupted. It was interesting to see what happened when somebody else, other than me, was in trouble for a change. Somebody was dispatched to find Mark, someone else alerted his parents, and yet another person argued with the two sheriff's deputies. Apparently, as Mark was only seventeen, there was some problem with letting the cops remove him from school grounds without his parents' permission.

After a while, Mark showed up, looking bewildered. He was a tall, good-looking guy, with dark hair and even darker eyes. Even though he played football, he didn't have a football player's thick neck or waist or anything. He was the team quarterback, which was why.

"What's up?" he said to the secretary, who darted a nervous look at Mr. Goodhart. He was still yelling at the sheriff's deputies, in his office.

"Um," the secretary said. "They aren't quite ready for you. Have a seat."

Mark took a seat on the orange vinyl couch across from mine. I studied him over the top of the Army brochure I was pretending to read. Most murder victims, I remembered seeing somewhere, know their killers. Had Mark strangled his girlfriend and dumped her body in Pike's Quarry? And if so, why? Was he some kind of sick pervert? Did he suffer from that killing rage they were always talking about on *America's Most Wanted?*

"Hey," Mark said to the secretary. "You got a water cooler in here?"

The secretary nervously admitted that they had, and pointed to its location, a little bit down the corridor. Mark got up to get a cup of water. I could not help noticing, from behind my brochure, that his 505s fit him very nicely.

On his way back from the water cooler, Mark noticed me and went, politely, "Oh, hey, sorry. Did you want one?"

I looked up from the brochure as if I were noticing him for the first time. "Who, me?" I asked. "Oh, no, thank you."

"Oh." Mark sat down again. "Okay." He finished all the water in his cup, crumpled it, looked around for a wastebasket, and, not seeing one, left the cup on the magazine-strewn table in front of us.

"So, what are you in for?" he asked me.

"I tried to choke Heather Montrose," I said.

"Really?" He grinned. "I've felt like doing that myself, coupla times."

I wanted to point out to him that this was something he'd be wise to keep from the sheriff, but didn't think I could do so in front of the secretary, who was busy pretending not to listen to our conversation.

"I mean, that Heather," Mark said. "She can be a real . . ." He politely refrained from swearing. A real Boy Scout, Mark Leskowski. "Well, you know."

"I *do* know," I said. "Listen. I'm sorry about Amber. She was your girlfriend, right?"

"Yeah." Mark's gaze strayed from my face to the center of the table between us. "Thanks."

The door to Mr. Goodhart's office opened, and he came out and spoke with forced joviality.

"Mark," he said. "Good to see you. Come in here a minute, will you? There are some folks here who want to have a word with you."

Mark nodded and stood up. As he did so, he wiped his hands nervously on the denim covering his thighs. When he took his hands away again, I saw damp spots where they'd been.

He was sweating, even though, with the air conditioning on full blast, I was a little chilly, in spite of my sweater set.

Mark Leskowski was nervous. Very nervous.

He looked down at me as he passed by my couch.

"Well," he said. "See you later."

"Sure," I said. "Later."

He went into Mr. Goodhart's office. Just before following Mark, Mr. Goodhart noticed I was still sitting there.

"Jessica," he said, jerking a thumb toward the door to the central hallway. "Out."

And so I left.

CHAPTER

3

"I figured it out," Ruth said as we drove home—with the top down—after school let out that day.

I was too distracted to reply, however, as we'd just sailed past the turnoff to Pike's Creek Road.

"Dude," I said. "You missed it."

"Missed what?" Ruth demanded, taking a healthy sip from the Diet Coke she'd picked up from the drive-through. Then she made a face. "Oh, God. You have *got* to be kidding me."

"It's not *that* far out of the way," I pointed out to her.

"You," Ruth said, "are never going to learn. Are you?"

"What?" I shrugged innocently. "What is so wrong about driving past his place of work?"

"I'll tell you what's wrong with it," Ruth said. "It is a direct violation of The Rules."

I snorted.

"I'm serious," Ruth said. "Boys don't like to be chased, Jess. They like to do the chasing."

"I am not chasing him," I said. "I am merely suggesting that we drive past the garage where he works."

"That," Ruth said, "is chasing him. As is calling him and hanging up when he answers." Oops. Guilty. "As is haunting the places he normally hangs out in, memorizing his schedule, and pretending to bump into him by mistake."

Guilty. Guilty. Guilty.

I snapped my seatbelt in irritation. "He'd never know we were swinging by just to see him," I said, "if you pretended like you needed an oil change or something."

"Would you," Ruth said, "get your mind off Rob Wilkins for five minutes and listen to me? I am trying to tell you, I think I figured out why everybody believes you still have psychic powers."

"Oh, yeah?" I was so not interested. It had been an exhausting day. It was bad enough a girl we knew had been murdered. The fact that people were going around blaming me for her death was even harder to take. "You know, Mark Leskowski actually offered me water today in the guidance office. If I were stranded in the desert, I would never have expected him to—"

"Karen Sue," Ruth said as we made the turn by Kroger's.

I looked around. "Where?"

"No. Karen Sue," Ruth said, "is the one going

around telling everyone you're still psychic. Suzy Choi told me she overheard Karen Sue telling everyone at the Thirty-one Flavors last Saturday night that, over the summer, you found this kid who'd gone missing inside a cave."

I forgot all about Rob. "I'll kill her," I said.

"I know." Ruth shook her head so that her blonde curls bounced. "And we thought we'd covered our tracks so well."

I couldn't believe it. Karen Sue and I had never exactly been friends, or anything, but that she'd out me so extremely . . . well, I was shocked.

I shouldn't have been *that* shocked, however. It *was* Karen Sue we were talking about, after all. The girl about whom my mother had, for years, asked, "Why can't you be more like her? Karen Sue never gets into fights, and she always wears whatever her mother tells her, and I've never heard that Karen Sue refused to go to church because she wanted to stay home to watch old *Battlestar Galactica* reruns."

Karen Sue Hankey. My mortal enemy.

"I'll kill her," I said, again.

"Well," Ruth said as she pulled into the driveway to my house, "I wouldn't suggest going to that extreme. But a firm lecture might be in order."

Right. I'd firm lecture her to death.

"Now," Ruth said. "What's this about Mark Leskowski?"

I told her about seeing Mark in the guidance office.

"That's awful," Ruth said when I was done.

"Mark and Amber were always so cute together. He loved her so much. How can the police possibly suspect that he had anything to do with her death?"

"I don't know," I said, remembering his sweaty palms. I'd left that part out when I'd repeated the story to Ruth. "Maybe he was the last person to see her or something."

"Maybe," Ruth said. "Hey, maybe his parents will hire my dad to represent Mark. You know, if the cops do charge with him anything."

"Yeah," I said. Ruth's dad was the best lawyer in town. "Maybe. Well. I better go." We'd gotten home so late the night before, I'd barely had a chance to say a word to my family. Another reason, I might add, I hadn't heard about Amber. "See you later."

"Later," Ruth said as I started to get out of the car. "Hey, what was that with Todd Mintz in the caf today, coming to your defense against Jeff Day?"

I looked at her blankly. "I don't know," I said. I hadn't actually realized that's what Todd had been doing, but now that I thought about it . . .

"I guess he hates Jeff as much as we do," I said, with a shrug.

Ruth laughed as she backed out of my driveway. "Yeah," she said. "That's probably why. And that miniskirt had nothing to do with it. I told you a makeover would do wonders for your social life."

She honked as she drove away, but she wasn't

going far. The Abramowitzes lived right next door.

Which was how, as I was going up the steps to the front door of my own house, I was able to hear Ruth's twin brother Skip call from his own front porch, "Hey, Mastriani. Want to come over later and let me beat you at Bandicoot?"

I leaned over and peered at Skip through the tall hedge that separated our two houses. Good God. It was bad enough I'd had to spend two weeks of my summer practically incarcerated with him. If he thought I was going to willingly extend my sentence, he had to be nuts.

"Uh," I called. "Can I take a rain check on that?"

"No problem," Skip hollered back.

Shuddering, I went inside.

And was greeted by someone even more frightening than Skip.

"Jessica," Great-aunt Rose said, intercepting me in the foyer before I had a chance to make a break for the stairs up to my room. "There you are. I was beginning to think I wouldn't get a chance to see you this trip." I had managed to elude her last night by getting home so late, and then again that morning, before school, by darting out of the house before breakfast. I had thought she'd be gone by the time I got home from school.

"Your father's driving me back to the airport," Great-aunt Rose went on, "in half an hour, you know."

Half an hour! If Ruth had just driven by the garage where Rob worked, like I asked, I might have been able to avoid Great-aunt Rose altogether this trip!

"Hi, Auntie," I said, bending down to give her a kiss on the cheek. Great-aunt Rose is the only member of my family I can honestly say I tower over. But that's only because osteoporosis has shrunk her down to about four foot eleven, an inch shorter than me.

"Well, let me look at you," Great-aunt Rose said, pushing me away. Her watery brown-eyed gaze ran over me critically from head to toe.

"Hmph," she said. "Nice to see you in a skirt for once. But don't you think it's a little short? They let girls go to school in skirts that short these days? Why, in my day, if I'd shown up in a skirt like that, I'd have been sent home to change!"

Poor Douglas. For two weeks he'd been sentenced to undiluted Great-aunt Rose. No wonder he'd feigned sleep the night before when I'd gotten home. I wouldn't have wanted to talk to a traitor like me, either.

"Toni!" Rose called, to my mother. "Come out here and look at what your daughter has got on. Is that how you're letting her dress these days?"

My mom, still looking sunburned and happy from her trip out east, from which she and my dad had only returned the day before, came into the foyer.

"Why, I think she looks fine," Mom said, taking in my ensemble with approval. "Far better than she used to dress last year, when I couldn't peel her out of jeans and a T-shirt."

"Um," I said, uncomfortably. I'd gotten as far as the landing, but didn't see how I was going to be able to sneak any farther upstairs without them noticing. "It was great to see you, Aunt Rose. Sorry you have to leave so soon. But I have a lot of homework—"

"Homework?" my mother said. "On the first day of school? Oh, I don't think so."

She'd seen through me, of course. My mom knew good and well how I felt about Great-aunt Rose. She just didn't want to be stuck with the old biddy herself. And she'd left Douglas alone with her for two weeks! Two weeks!

Talk about cruel and unusual punishment.

Then again, if she'd been counting on Great-aunt Rose keeping an eagle eye on him, she couldn't have found anyone better. Nothing got past Great-aunt Rose.

"Is that lipstick you're wearing, Jessica?" Great-aunt Rose demanded when we got out of the darkness of the foyer and into the brightly lit kitchen.

"Um," I said. "No. Cherry Chap Stick."

"Lipstick!" Great-aunt Rose cried in disgust. "Lipstick and miniskirts! No wonder all of those boys kept calling while you were away. They probably think you're easy."

I raised my eyebrows at this. "Really? Boys called me?" I'd known, of course, that girls had

called—Heather Montrose, among others. But I
hadn't known any boys had phoned. "Were any
of them named Rob?"

"I didn't ask their names," Great-aunt Rose
said. "I told them never to call here again. I
explained that you weren't that kind of girl."

I said an expletive that caused my mother to
throw me a warning look. Fortunately, Great-
aunt Rose didn't hear it, as she was still too busy
talking.

"An emergency, they kept calling it," she said.
"Had to get in touch with you right away,
because of some emergency. Ridiculous. You
know what kind of emergencies teenagers have,
of course. They'd probably run out of Cherry
Coke down at the local soda shop."

I looked at Great-aunt Rose very hard as I said,
"Actually, a girl from my class got kidnapped.
One of the cheerleaders. They found her yesterday, floating in one of the quarries. She'd been
strangled."

My mother looked startled. "Oh, my God,"
she said. "That girl? The one I read about in the
paper this morning? You knew her?"

Parents. I swear.

"I've only sat behind her," I said, "in homeroom every year since the sixth grade."

"Oh, no." My mom had her hands on her face.
"Her poor parents. They must be devastated.
We'd better send over a platter."

Restauranteurs. That's how they think. Any
crisis, and it's always, "Let's send over a platter."

Last spring, when half our town's police force had been camped out in our front yard, holding off the hordes of reporters who wanted to score an interview with Lightning Girl, all my mom had been able to think about was making sure we had enough biscotti to go around.

Great-aunt Rose wasn't nearly as upset as my mom. She went, "Cheerleader? Serves her right. Prancing around in those little short skirts. You better watch out, Jessica, or you'll be next."

"Aunt Rose!" my mom cried.

"Well," Great-aunt Rose said, with a sniff. "It could happen. Particularly if you let her continue to wear outfits like that." She nodded at my ensemble.

I decided I had had enough visiting. I got up and said, "It's been swell seeing you again, Auntie, but I think I'll go up and say hi to Douglas. He was asleep when I got home last night, so—"

"Douglas," Great-aunt Rose said with a roll of her rheumy eyes. "When *isn't* he asleep?"

Which gave me a clue as to how Douglas had borne Great-aunt Rose's company for the two weeks he'd been alone with her. Feigning sleep.

He was still at it when I burst into his room a minute later.

"Douglas," I said, looking down at him from the side of his bed. "Give it up. I know you're not really asleep."

He opened one eye. "Is she gone?" he asked.

"Almost," I said. "Dad's coming to pick her up

and take her to the airport in a few minutes. Mom wants you to come down and say good-bye."

Douglas moaned and pulled a pillow over his head.

"Just kidding," I said, sinking down onto the bed beside him. "I think Mom's getting a dose of what you must have had to put up with this whole time. I don't believe Great-aunt Rose will be invited back any time soon."

"The horror," Douglas said from beneath the pillow. "The horror."

"Yeah," I said. "But hey, it's over now. How are you doing?"

Douglas said, his voice still muffled by the pillow, "Well, I didn't slash my wrists this time, did I? So I must be doing okay."

I digested this. The reason Douglas, at twenty years of age, could not be trusted to stay in the house alone for two weeks is because of his tendency to hear voices inside his head. The voices are held pretty much at bay with the help of medication, but occasionally Douglas still has episodes. That's what his doctors call it when he listens to the voices, and then does what they tell him to do, which is generally something bad, like, oh, I don't know, kill himself.

Episodes.

"I'll tell you what," he said from beneath the pillow. "I almost episoded Great-aunt Rose, is what I almost did."

"Really?" Too bad he hadn't. I might have gotten the message about Amber being missing in time to have saved her. "What about the Feds? Any sign of them?"

The Federal Bureau of Investigation, like my classmates, refuses to believe I am no longer psychic. They were mightily taken with me last spring, when word got out about my "special ability." They were so taken with me, in fact, that they decided to enlist my aid in locating some unsavory individuals on their most wanted list. They forgot one slight detail, however: to *ask* me if I wanted to work for them.

Which of course I did not. It took all sorts of unpleasantness—including lying that I no longer have any psychic powers—to extricate myself from their clutches. Since then, they had taken to following me around, waiting for me to slip up, at which point I suppose they will point their finger and yell, "Liar, liar, pants on fire."

At least, that's all I hope they'll do.

Douglas pushed the pillow away and sat up. "No white vans mysteriously parked across the street since you took off for camp," he said. "Except for Rose, it's been downright restful around here. I mean, with both you and Mike gone."

We were quiet for a minute, thinking about Mike. Across the hall, his bedroom door stood open, and I could see that his computer, all of his books, and his telescope were gone. They were sitting in some dorm room at Harvard now. Mike would be torturing his new roommate, instead of Douglas and me, with his obsession over Claire Lippman, the cute redhead into whose bedroom window Mike had spent so many hours peering.

"It's going to be weird with him gone," Douglas said.

"Yeah," I said. But actually, I wasn't thinking about Mike. I was thinking about Amber. Claire Lippman, the girl Mike had loved from afar for a few years now, spent almost all of her free time in the summer tanning herself at the quarries. Had she, I wondered, seen Amber there, before the crime that had taken her life?

"What," Douglas asked a second later, "are you so dressed up for, anyway?"

I looked down at myself in surprise. "Oh," I said. "School."

"School?" Douglas seemed shocked. "Since when have you ever bothered dressing up for school?"

"I'm turning over a new leaf," I informed him. "No more jeans, no more T-shirts, no more fighting, no more detention."

"Interesting corollary," Douglas said. "Equating jeans with fighting and detention. But I'll bite. Did it work?"

"Not exactly," I said, and told him about my day, leaving out the part about what Heather had said concerning him.

When I was through, Doug whistled, low and long.

"So they're blaming you," he said. "Even

though you couldn't possibly have known anything about it?"

"Hey," I said with a shrug. "Amber was in with the popular crowd, and popular kids are not popular for their ability to objectively reason. Just for their looks, mainly. Or maybe their ability to suck up."

"Jeez," Douglas said. "What are you going to do?"

"What *can* I do?" I asked with a shrug. "I mean, she's dead."

"Couldn't you—I don't know. Couldn't you summon up a picture of her killer? Like in your mind's eye? Like if you really concentrated?"

"Sorry," I said in a flat voice. "It doesn't work like that."

Unfortunately. My psychic ability does not extend itself toward anything other than addresses. Seriously. Show me a picture of anyone, and that night, I'll dream up the person's most current location. But precognitive indications of the lottery numbers? No. Visions of plane crashes, or impending national doom? Nothing. All I can do is locate missing people. And I can only do that in my sleep.

Well, most of the time, anyway. There'd been a strange incident over the summer when I'd managed to summon up someone's location just by hugging his pillow. . . .

But that, I remained convinced, had been a fluke.

"Oh," Douglas said suddenly, leaning over to

pull something out from beneath his bed. "By the way, I was in charge of collecting the Abramowitzes' mail while they were away, and I took the liberty of relieving them of this." He presented me with a large brown envelope that had been addressed to Ruth. "From your friend at 1-800-WHERE-R-YOU, I believe?"

I took the envelope and opened it. Inside—as there was every week, mailed to Ruth, since I suspected the Feds were going through my mail, just waiting for something like this to prove I'd been lying to them when I'd said I was no longer psychic—was a note from my operative at the missing children's organization—Rosemary—and a photo of a kid she had determined was really and truly missing . . . not a runaway, who might be missing by choice, or a kid who'd been stolen by his non-custodial parent, who might be better off where he was. But an actual, genuinely missing kid.

I looked at the picture—of a little Asian girl, with buckteeth and butterfly hair clips—and sighed. Amber Mackey, who'd sat in front of me in homeroom every day for six years, might be dead. But for the rest of us, life goes on.

Yeah. Try telling that to Amber's parents.

CHAPTER 4

When I woke up the next morning, I knew two things: One, that Courtney Hwang was living on Baker Street in San Francisco. And two, that I was going to take the bus to school that day.

Don't ask me what one had to do with the other. My guess would be a big fat nothing.

But if I took the bus to school, I'd have an opportunity that I wouldn't if I let Ruth drive me to school in her Cabriolet: I'd be able to talk to Claire Lippman, and find out what she knew about the activities at the quarry just before Amber went missing.

I called Ruth first. My call to Rosemary would have to wait until I found a phone that no one could connect me to, if 1-800-WHERE-R-YOU happened to trace the call. Which they did every call they got, actually.

"You want to take the bus," Ruth repeated, incredulously.

"It's nothing against the Cabriolet," I assured her. "It's just that I want to have a word with Claire."

"You want to take the bus," Ruth said again.

"Seriously, Ruth," I said. "It's just a one-time thing. I just want to ask Claire a few questions about what was up at the quarry the night Amber disappeared."

"Fine," Ruth said. "Take the bus. See if I care. What have you got on?"

"What?"

"On your body. What are you wearing on your body?"

I looked down at myself. "Olive khaki mini, beige crocheted tank with matching three-quarter-sleeve cardigan, and beige espadrilles."

"The platforms?"

"Yes."

"Good," Ruth said, and hung up.

Fashion is *hard*. I don't know how those popular girls do it. At least my hair, being extremely short and sort of spiky, didn't have to be blow-dried and styled. That would just about kill me, I think.

Claire was sitting on the stoop of the house where the bus picked up the kids in our neighborhood. I live in the kind of neighborhood where people don't mind if you do this. Sit on their stoop, I mean, while waiting for the bus.

Claire was eating an apple and reading what looked to be a script. Claire, a senior, was the reigning leading lady of Ernie Pyle High's drama club. In the bright morning sunlight, her red bob shined. She had definitely blow-dried and styled just minutes before.

Ignoring all the freshmen geeks and car-less rejects that were gathered on the sidewalk, I said, "Hi, Claire."

She looked up, squinting in the sun. Then she swallowed what she'd been chewing and said, "Oh, hi, there, Jess. What are you doing here?"

"Oh, nothing," I said, sitting down on the step beneath the one she'd appropriated. "Ruth had to leave early, is all." I prayed Ruth wouldn't drive by as I said this, and that if she did, she wouldn't tootle the horn, as she was prone to when we passed what we've always considered the rejects at the bus stop.

"Huh," Claire said. She glanced admiringly down at my bare leg. "You've got a great tan. How'd you get it?"

Claire Lippman has always been obsessed with tanning. It was because of this obsession, actually, that my brother Mike had become obsessed with her. She spent almost every waking hour of the summer months on the roof of her house, sunbathing . . . except when she could get someone to drive her to the quarries. Swimming in the quarries was, of course, against the law, which was why everyone did it, Claire Lippman more than anyone. Though, as a red-head, her hobby must have been a particularly frustrating one for her, since it took almost a whole summer of exposure to turn her skin even the slightest shade darker. Sitting beside her, I felt a little like Pocahontas. Pocahontas hanging out with The Little Mermaid.

"I worked as a camp counselor," I explained to her. "And then Ruth and I spent two weeks at the dunes, up at Lake Michigan."

"You're lucky," Claire said wistfully. "I've just been stuck at the stupid quarries all summer."

Pleased by this smooth entré into the subject I'd been longing to discuss with her, I started to say, "Hey, yeah, that's right. You must have been there, then, the day Amber Mackey went missing—"

That's what I started to say, anyway. I didn't get a chance to finish, however. That was because, to my utter disbelief, a red Trans Am pulled up to the bus stop, and Ruth's twin brother Skip leaned out of the T-top to call, "Jess! Hey, Jess! What are you doing here? D'ju and Ruth have another fight?"

All the geeks—the backpack patrol, Ruth and I called them, because of their enormous, well, backpacks—turned to look at me. There is nothing, let me tell you, more humiliating than being stared at by a bunch of fourteen-year-old boys.

I had no choice but to call back to Skip, "No, Ruth and I did not get into a fight. I just felt like riding the bus today."

Really, in the history of the bus stop, had anyone ever uttered anything as lame as that?

"Don't be an idiot," Skip said. "Get in the car. I'll drive you."

All the nerds, who'd been staring at Skip while

he spoke, turned their heads to look expectantly at me.

"Um," I said, feeling my cheeks heating up and thankful my tan hid my blush. "No, thanks, Skip. Claire and I are talking."

"Claire can come, too." Skip ducked back inside the car, leaned over, and threw open the passenger door. "Come on."

Claire was already gathering up her books.

"Great!" she squealed. "Thanks!"

I followed more reluctantly. This was so not what I'd had in mind.

"Come on, Claire," Skip was saying as I approached the car. "You can get in back—"

I saw Claire, who was a willowy five-foot-nine if she was an inch, hesitate while looking into the cramped recesses of Skip's backseat. With a sigh, I said, "I'll get in back."

When I was wedged into the dark confines of the Trans Am's rear seat, Claire threw the passenger seat back and climbed in.

"This is so sweet of you, Skip," she said, checking out her reflection in his rearview mirror. "Thanks a lot. The bus is okay, and all, but, you know. This is much better."

"Oh," Skip said, fastening his seatbelt. "I know. You all right back there?" he asked me.

"Fine," I said. I had, I knew, to turn the conversation back to the subject of the quarries. But how?

"Great." Skip threw the car into gear and we were off, leaving the geeks in our dust. Actually, that part I sort of enjoyed.

"So," Skip said, "how are you ladies this morning?"

See? This is the problem with Skip. He says things like "So, how are you ladies this morning?" How are you supposed to take a guy who says things like that seriously? Skip's not ugly, or anything—he looks a lot like Ruth, actually: a chubby blond in glasses. Only, of course, Skip doesn't have breasts.

Still, Skip just isn't dream date material, despite the Trans Am.

Too bad he hasn't seemed to figure that out yet.

"I'm fine," Claire said. "How about you, Jess?"

"I'm fine," I said, from the manger-sized backseat. Then I took the plunge. "What were you saying, Claire? About being at the quarry the day Amber disappeared?"

"Oh," Claire said. The wind through the T-top was unstyling her bob, but Claire didn't appear to care. She ran her fingers through it delightedly. You don't get that kind of fresh air on the bus.

"My God, what a nightmare *that* was. We'd all just been hanging out, you know, all day. No big deal. Some of those guys from the football team, they brought a grill, and they were barbecuing, and everyone was, you know, pretty drunk, even though I warned them they'd get dehydrated, drinking beer in the sun—" For someone whose primary goal was to bake her skin to a crisp, Claire had always been surprisingly health-conscious. One of the reasons it took her so long to achieve the tan she wanted each summer was that she insisted on slathering herself with SPF 15.

"And then the sun went down, and some people started packing up their stuff to, you know, go home. And that's when Mark—Leskowski, you know? He and Amber were going out for, like, ever. Anyway, he was all, 'Has anybody seen Amber?' And we all started looking for her, through the woods, you know, and then, thinking maybe she'd tripped or something, in the water. I mean, we thought maybe she'd fallen in, or something. The drop's pretty steep. When we couldn't find her, we figured, well, she must have gone home with somebody else, or whatever. We didn't say that to *Mark*, of course, but that's what we were all thinking."

Claire turned to look at me, her pretty blue eyes troubled. "But then she never came home. And the next day, as soon as it was light, we all went back to the quarry, you know, to look for her."

"But you didn't," I said, "find anything."

"Not that day. Her body didn't show up until Sunday morning." Claire went on, "A bunch of people tried to call you, you know. Hoping you could help find her. This one girl, Karen Sue Hankey, she says you found some kid over the summer who'd been lost in a cave, so we thought maybe you still had, you know, that whole psychic thing going—"

That psychic thing. That was one way of putting it, anyway.

I was seriously going to kill Karen Sue Hankey.

"I wasn't exactly reachable last weekend," I said. "I was up at—" I broke off, noticing we were approaching the turnoff to Pike's Creek Road. "Hey, Skip, turn here."

Skip obediently took the turn. "And I'm turning here because?"

"I want, um, a cruller," I said, since there was a Dunkin' Donuts near the garage where Rob worked.

"Ooh," Claire said. "Crullers. Yum. You don't get crullers on the bus."

When we buzzed past Rob's uncle's garage, I sank down real low in the seat, so in case Rob was outside, he wouldn't see me.

Rob was outside, and he didn't see me. He was bent inside the hood of an Audi, his soft dark hair falling forward over his square-jawed face, his jeans looking properly snug and faded in all the right places. It was warm out, even though it wasn't quite eight in the morning yet, and Rob had on a short-sleeved shirt, revealing his nicely pronounced triceps.

It had been nearly three weeks since I'd last seen him. He'd shown up at the Wawasee All-Camp recital, where I'd had a solo. I'd been surprised . . . I hadn't expected him to come four hours, one way, just to hear me play.

And then, since I had to go out with my parents afterwards—and let's face it, my parents would not approve of Rob, a guy with a criminal record who comes, as they say in books, from the wrong side of the tracks—he just had to get back on his bike afterward and drive four hours home. That's a long way to go, just to hear some girl you aren't even going out with play a nocturne on her flute.

It got me thinking. You know, since he'd driven so far to hear me play. Maybe he liked me after all, in spite of the whole jailbait thing.

Except, of course, that I'd been back two days already, and he still hadn't called.

Anyway, that brief glimpse of Rob, checking that Audi's oil, was all I was probably going to see of him for a while, so I watched until we pulled into the parking lot of the Dunkin' Donuts and I couldn't see him anymore.

Hey, I know it was uncool to be scoping on boys at the same time as I was trying to solve a murder. But Nancy Drew still had time to date Ned Nickerson, didn't she, in between solving all those mysteries?

Except of course, Ned wasn't on probation, and I don't think any of those mysteries Nancy solved involved a dead cheerleader.

While Skip and Claire went to the counter to get crullers, I said I had to make a call. Then I went to the payphone by the door to the rest-room and dialed 1-800-WHERE-R-YOU.

Rosemary was glad to hear from me, even though of course we had to keep the call brief. Rosemary is totally risking her job, doing what she does for me. You know, sending me those photos and reports on missing kids. Those files aren't supposed to leave the office.

But I guess Rosemary thinks it is worth it, if even one kid gets found. And since we've started working together, we've found a lot of kids, between the two of us. We kind of have to cool it, of course, so no one gets too suspicious. We average about a kid a week, which, let me tell you, is way better than 1-800-WHERE-R-YOU was doing before I came along.

The good thing about working with Rosemary, as opposed to like the FBI or the police or something, is that Rosemary is totally discreet and would never, say, call the *National Enquirer* and have them come to my house to interview me. Having too many reporters around has a tendency to send Douglas into an episode. That is why I lied last spring, and told everyone I didn't have my psychic powers anymore.

And up until recently, everyone believed it.

Everyone except Karen Sue Hankey, apparently.

Anyway, after Rosemary and I were through chatting, I hung up, and walked out to find Skip telling Claire about the time in third grade when he and I shot his GI Joe into space using a lead pipe and gunpowder extracted from about three hundred Blackcats. I noticed that he left out the part about putting a Roman candle inside my Barbie's head, an act about which I had not been consulted and which had not been part of our space shuttle program as I'd understood it. Also the part where we nearly blew ourselves up.

"Wow," Claire said as she licked sugar off her fingertips. "I always saw you two hanging out together, but I never knew you did cool stuff like that."

"Oh, yeah," I overheard Skip say. "Jess and I go way back. *Way* back."

Hello. What was *this* all about? Just because I'd spent two weeks hanging out with the guy at his parents' lakehouse did not mean I wanted to renew a relationship that had been formed due to a mutual love of explosives and which had disintegrated as soon as our parents discovered our illicit hobby and took away all our firecrackers. Skip and I had nothing in common. Nothing except our past.

"Ready to go?" Skip asked brightly as I came up to their table. "We better get a move on, or we'll be late for homeroom."

Homeroom. I forgot all about my annoyance with Skip.

"Hey, Claire," I asked her as we headed back toward the car. "That Friday Amber disappeared. Did she and Mark Leskowski hang out with the rest of you the whole day, or did they ever go off by themselves?"

"Are you kidding?" Claire tossed her copper-colored curls, which, in spite of having become windblown, still looked fresh and pretty. Claire was that kind of girl. "Those two were inseparable. I mean, Mark sits in front of me first period, and let me tell you, it was like he had to pry himself out of that girl's arms. . . ."

I raised my eyebrows. No wonder Amber had never made it into her seat before the first bell.

"What about the day she disappeared?" I asked. "Were they still . . . inseparable."

Claire nodded. "Oh, yeah. They were all over each other. We were joking about how they were going to come down with some serious poison ivy, what with the number of trips they took into the woods with each other in order to 'be alone.'"

I climbed into the backseat. "And that last time they went off together, to be alone—was that how Mark came back?"

Claire plopped down into the passenger seat. "What do you mean?"

"I mean, did he come back alone?"

Claire tilted her head to one side as she thought about it. Beside her, Skip started up the car. I wondered what Rob, back at the garage, would think if he'd known I'd driven right by him and hadn't even said hi.

"You know," Claire said, "I can't imagine that he did. Come back alone, I mean. I wasn't paying that close attention—those guys aren't really my crowd, you know? I mean, that whole cheerleading, football thing. That is so not my scene. I mean, if they gave just half the amount of money to support the drama department as they do the athletics department, we could put on a *lot* better shows. We could have rented costumes, instead of making them ourselves, and we could get mikes so we don't have to scream to be heard in the back row—"

I could see that Claire was slipping off track. To steer her back to the subject at hand, I said, "You're right. It isn't fair. Somebody should do something. So you didn't see Mark come back alone from any of his and Amber's trips into the woods together?"

"No," Claire said. "I don't think so. I mean, somebody would have said something if Mark had come back alone. Don't you think? Don't you think somebody would have said 'Hey, Mark, where's Amber?'"

"You'd think so," Skip said.

"Yes," I said, thoughtfully. "Wouldn't you?"

CHAPTER

5

They held Amber Mackey's memorial service later that day. Instead of having it in a church or a funeral home or whatever, they had it in the gym.

That's right. The gym of Ernest Pyle High School.

And they had it during seventh period. Attendance was mandatory. The only person who was not there, actually, was Amber. I guess Principal Feeney drew the line at letting Amber's parents drag her coffin out in front of all two thousand of their daughter's peers.

The band played a slowed-down rendition of the school song, I guess so it would sound sad. Then Principal Feeney got up and talked about what a great person Amber had been. I doubt he had ever even met her, but whatever. He looked good in the dark gray suit he'd donned for the occasion.

When the principal was done talking, Coach Albright came out and said a few words. Coach Albright is not known for his eloquence as a speaker, so fortunately he didn't say much. He just announced that his players would be wearing black armbands on their uniforms for the season in honor of Amber. Never having been to a sporting event at my school, I had no idea what he was talking about until Ruth explained it to me.

Then Mrs. Tidd, the cheerleading coach, got up and said a bunch of stuff about how much they were going to miss Amber, especially when it came to her ability to do standing back tucks. Then she said that, in honor of Amber, both the varsity and junior varsity cheerleading squads had put together an interpretive dance.

Then—and I kid you not—the cheerleaders and Pompettes did this dance, in the middle of the gym floor, to Celine Dion's "My Heart Will Go On," from *Titanic*.

And people *cried* during it. I swear. I looked around, and people were totally crying.

It was a good dance and all. You could tell they'd worked totally hard on it. And they'd only had like two days or something to memorize it.

Still, it didn't make me feel like crying. Seriously. And I don't think I'm like a hardened person or anything. I just hope that when I die, nobody does an interpretive dance at my memorial service. I can't stand that kind of thing.

I can tell you what did make me feel like crying,

though. The fact that, as the dance was going on, some people walked into the gym. I was sitting midway up the bleachers—Ruth wanted to make sure we could see everything, and she hadn't even known, at the time, that there was going to be an interpretive dance—but I could still make out their features. Well enough to know they weren't high-school students.

They weren't high-school teachers, either.

What they were was Feds.

Seriously. And not just any Feds, either, but my old friends Special Agents Johnson and Smith.

You would think that, by now, they'd have given up. I mean, they've been following me around since May, and they still don't have anything solid to pin on me. Not like what I'm doing is even wrong. I mean, okay, yeah, I help reunite missing kids with their families. Oooh, lock me up. I'm a dangerous criminal.

Except of course they don't want to lock me up. They want me to work for them.

But I have a real problem with working for an institution that routinely railroads people who might conceivably be innocent of the crimes with which they've been accused, just like *The Fugitive*. . . .

And apparently it wasn't enough, my telling them I no longer had the power to find missing people. Oh, no. They have to tap my phone, and read my mail, and follow me all the way to Lake Wawasee.

And now they have the nerve to show up at a

memorial service for one of my dead friends. . . .

And yeah, okay, Amber wasn't really my friend, but I sat behind her for like half an hour every single weekday for six years. That has to count for something, right?

"I'm outta here," I said to Ruth as I started gathering up my things.

"What do you mean, you're outta here?" Ruth demanded, looking alarmed. "You can't leave. It's an assembly."

"Watch me," I said.

"They've got student council members posted at all the exits," Ruth whispered.

"That's not all they got posted by the exits," I said, and pointed at Special Agents Johnson and Smith, who were talking to Principal Feeney off to one side of the gym.

"Oh, God," Ruth breathed, when she saw them. "Not again."

"Oh, yes," I said. "And if you think I'm sticking around here to get the third degree about Courtney Hwang, which is for sure why they're here, you got another think coming, sister. See you around."

Without another word, I inched my way over to the far end of the bleacher—past a number of people who gave me dirty looks as I went by, though because I'd stepped on their toes, not because they were mad at me about Amber—until I'd reached the gap between the bleachers and the wall. This I slithered through without any major difficulty—although my landing, in my platform espadrilles, was no ten-pointer, let me tell you. After that, it was an easy stroll beneath the bleachers to the nearest door, where I planned to fake an illness and be given leave to make my way to the nurse's office. . . .

Except of course when I emerged from beneath the bleachers and saw the student council member guarding that particular exit, I knew I wouldn't have to fake an illness.

No, I felt pretty genuinely sick.

"Jessica," Karen Sue Hankey said, clutching the pile of *Remember Amber* booklets she'd handed out to each of us as we filed in. The booklet, four pages long, had color copies of photos of Amber in various cheerleader poses, interposed with the printed lyrics to "My Heart Will Go On." Most people, I'd noticed as I'd made my way beneath the bleachers, had dropped theirs.

"What are you doing?" Karen Sue hissed. "Get back to your seat. It's not over yet."

I clutched my stomach. Not enough to draw attention to myself. The last thing I wanted was for Special Agents Johnson and Smith to notice me. But enough to get the point across.

"Karen Sue," I hiccuped. "I think I'm going to—"

I stumbled past her and dove through the doors. They let out into the music wing. Free. I was free! Now all I had to do was make my way to the student parking lot, and wait for Ruth to get to her car when they let everybody out. I might even get a chance to stretch out on her hood and work on my tan.

Except that Karen Sue followed me into the hallway, throwing a definite crimp in my plans.

"You are not sick, Jessica Mastriani," she said firmly. "You are faking it. You do the exact same thing in PE every time Mrs. Tidd announces the Presidential Fitness tests."

I couldn't believe this. It's not enough she has to go around outing me as a psychic to everyone. No, Karen Sue has to bar my escape from the Feds who are after me, too.

But I was not about to let my anger get the best of me. No way. I'd turned over a new leaf. It was already day two of the new school year, and guess what? I did not have detention.

And I was not going to ruin this excellent record by letting Karen Sue Hankey get under my skin.

"Karen Sue," I said, straightening up. "You're right. I'm not sick. But there are some people out there I don't want to see, if it's all the same to you. So could you please be a human being"—I barely restrained myself from adding, *for once in your life*—"and let me go?"

"Who do you not want to see?" Karen Sue wanted to know.

"Some Feds, if you must know. You see, I've had a lot of problems with people thinking I still have psychic powers, when in fact"—I added this last part with all the emphasis I could muster—"*I do not.*"

"You are such a liar, Jess," Karen Sue said, shaking her head so that her honey-blonde hair, the ends of which curled into perfect flips just above her shoulders, swung. "You know you found that Shane kid at camp this summer, when he got lost inside that cave."

"Yeah, I found him," I said. "But not because I'd had a psychic vision he was there or anything. Just because I had a hunch he'd been in there. That's all."

"Is that so?" Karen Sue looked prim. "Well, what you call a hunch, I call ESP. You have a gift from God, Jessica Mastriani, and that makes it a sin for you to try to deny it."

The problem, of course, is that Karen Sue goes to my church. She's been in my Sunday school class since forever.

The other problem is that Karen Sue is a goody-two-shoes suck-up we used to lock in the janitor's closet whenever the Sunday school teacher didn't show up on time. Which happened quite often, actually.

"Look, Karen Sue," I said. It was getting harder to repress my urge to knock those booklets out of her arms and grind her face into them. "I appreciate everything you've tried to do for me, in the name of the Lord and all, but could you just once try that whole turning-the-other-cheek thing—turn it toward the wall so you don't see me while I get the hell out of here? That way, if anyone asks, you won't be lying when you say you didn't see where I went."

Karen Sue looked at me sadly. "No," she said, and started for the door, clearly to seek the aid of someone larger than she was in detaining me.

I grabbed her wrist. But I wasn't going to hurt her. I swear I wasn't. I'd turned over a new leaf. I was in a brand new crocheted sweater set and espadrilles. I had on cherry Chap Stick. Girls dressed like me do not get into fights. Girls dressed like me reason with one another, in a friendly manner.

"Karen Sue," I said. "The thing is, the whole thing with the psychic power and all, it really upsets my brother Douglas, you know? I mean, the reporters coming around the house and calling and all of that. So you can see why I want to kind of keep it a secret, right? I mean, because of my brother."

Karen Sue's gaze never left mine as she wrenched her wrist from my hand.

"Your brother Douglas," she said, "is sick. His sickness is obviously a judgment from God. If Douglas went to church more often, and prayed harder, he would get better. And your denying your God-given gifts isn't helping. In fact, you are probably making him worse."

Well. What could I say to that?

Nothing, really. I mean, something like that, there's no appropriate response.

No appropriate *verbal* response, that is.

Karen Sue's screams brought Principal Feeney, Coach Albright, Mrs. Tidd, most of the student council, and Special Agents Johnson and Smith running. When she saw Karen Sue, Special Agent Smith got on her cell phone and called an ambulance.

But I guarantee her nose isn't even broken. She probably only burst a blood vessel or two.

As Principal Feeney and Special Agent Johnson led me away, I called out, "Hey, Karen Sue, maybe if you pray hard enough, God'll make the bleeding stop."

Taken out of context, I could see how this might sound callous. But none of them had heard what Karen Sue had said to me. And no amount of me going, "But she said—" seemed to impress upon them the fact that I was completely justified in my behavior.

"And I thought you'd been making some real progress," Mr. Goodhart said sadly when I was dragged into the guidance office.

"I *was* making progress." I threw myself onto one of the orange couches. "I'd like to see how long you could put up with Karen Sue's *stuff* before hauling off and slugging her."

Only I didn't say *"stuff."*

"I'll tell you one thing," Mr. Goodhart said. "I wouldn't let a girl like that push my buttons."

"She said it's my fault Douglas is sick," I said. "She said his sickness is a punishment from God for me not using my gift!"

Special Agent Johnson, who'd been sequestered away with Principal Feeney—consulting about me, I was sure—chose this moment to emerge from the principal's office.

"Really, Jessica," he said, sounding surprised. "I wouldn't have thought you'd be susceptible to that sort of nonsense."

"Well, if I am," I said, "it's because you're making me. Following me around all the time. Showing up at school. Badgering me. Well, I had nothing to do with finding that girl in San Francisco. Nothing!"

Special Agent Johnson raised his eyebrows. "I wasn't aware a girl in San Francisco had been found," he said mildly. "But thank you for letting me know."

I eyed him. "You . . . you aren't here about Courtney Hwang?"

"Contrary to what you apparently believe, Jessica," Special Agent Johnson said, "the world, much less my job, does not revolve around you. Jill and I are here for something quite unrelated to you."

The door to the guidance office opened, and Special Agent Smith came in.

"Well," she said. "That was exciting. The next time, Jessica, you feel the need to plunge your fist into a girl's face, please do it when I'm not around."

I looked from her to Special Agent Johnson and then back again.

"Wait a minute," I said. "If you two aren't here because of me, what are you here for?"

The door to the guidance office opened yet again, and this time, Mark Leskowski walked in, looking bewildered and strangely vulnerable for a guy who, at six feet tall, probably tips the scales at one eighty.

"You wanted to see me again, Mr. Goodhart?" Mark asked.

Mr. Goodhart glanced at Special Agents Johnson and Smith.

"Uh," he said. "Yes, Mark, I did. Actually, these, um, officers here wanted a word with you. But before you meet with him, um, officers, can I just have a word with you?"

Special Agent Johnson smiled. "Certainly," he said, and he and Special Agent Smith disappeared into Mr. Goodhart's office, and closed the door behind them.

Incredible. More than incredible. Indescribable. I punch Karen Sue Hankey in the face and get summoned to the guidance office for disciplinary action, *only to be forgotten about?*

What's more, my two archenemies, Special Agents Johnson and Smith, show up at Ernest Pyle High School, not to give *me* a hard time, but *someone else?*

Amber Mackey's murder had done a lot more than rob us of Amber. It had turned the universe as I had once known it upside down and backward.

This became even more apparent when Mark Leskowski—quarterback, senior class vice-president, and all-around hottie—smiled down at me—*me*, Jessica Mastriani, who's spent almost more time in detention than she has in class—and said, "Well. We meet again, I guess."

Oh, yeah. Call the Pentagon. Someone's gone and created a new world order.

CHAPTER

6

"So," Mark Leskowski said to me. "What are you in for this time?"

I looked at him. He was so beautiful. Not as beautiful as Rob Wilkins, of course, but then what guy was?

Still, Mark Leskowski was a close second in the dreamy department.

"I punched Karen Sue Hankey in the face," I said.

"Whoa." He actually looked impressed. "Good for you."

"You think so?" I asked. I can't tell you how good it felt, having the approval of a guy who looked that good in a pair of 505s. Seriously. Most of what I did on a regular basis, it seemed, Rob didn't approve of. Primarily because he was afraid it was going to get me killed, but still. He didn't have to be so bossy about it.

"Heck, yeah," Mark said. "That girl's such a wannabe, it hurts."

My God! My feelings about Karen Sue exactly! And yet somehow, when expressed through a set of such masculine lips, they seemed to have more validity than ever.

"Yeah," I said. "Yeah, she is, isn't she?"

"Is she! I'll tell you what. Amber used to call her the Klingon. You know, because she was always clinging onto the rest of us, trying to get in with the in crowd."

His mention of Amber snapped me back into reality. What was I doing? What was I doing, sitting on an orange vinyl couch in the guidance office, lusting after Mark Leskowski? He was being pulled in for questioning by the FBI. The FBI! That was some serious stuff.

"So," I said, my gaze darting toward the glass window in Mr. Goodhart's office door. Through it, I could see Special Agent Johnson speaking rapidly. Mr. Goodhart was Mark Leskowski's guidance counselor, as well as mine. Mr. Goodhart had all the Ls through Ps.

Mark noticed the direction of my gaze and nodded. "I guess I'm in some trouble now, huh?"

I said carefully, "Well, you know. If they're bringing in the FBI . . ."

"They always do," he said. "In cases of kidnapping. Or at least, that's what Mr. Goodhart says. Those two in there are the regional operatives."

Special Agents Johnson and Smith, regional

operatives? Really? It had never occurred to me that Allan and Jill might actually have homes. I had always pictured them living out of skanky motel rooms. But of course it made sense that they lived in the area. I heaved a shudder at the idea that I might one day bump into one of them at the grocery store.

"They are classifying what happened to Amber as a kidnapping/murder," Mark went on, "because Amber was . . . alive for a while before she got killed."

"Oh," I said. "Shouldn't you . . . I don't know. Have a lawyer, or something?"

"I have one," he said, looking down at his hands resting between his thighs. "He's on his way. My parents, too. I thought I had explained it all to the sheriff, but I guess . . . I don't know. I'm going to have to do it again. With those guys."

I followed his gaze. Now Mr. Goodhart was speaking to Special Agent Johnson. I couldn't see Special Agent Smith. She was probably sitting in my chair, the one by the window. I wondered if she was looking out at the car wash, the way I always did when I sat there.

"I just don't get it," Mark said, staring at a spot in the center of the coffee table between us, at a brochure that had I'M AN ARMY OF ONE written on it. "I mean, I loved Amber. I would never hurt her."

I glanced at the secretary. She was totally listening, but she was pretending not to, seeming to be very absorbed in a game of Minesweeper. She would click a button on her keyboard if Principal Feeney wandered this way, and the computer game would disappear, to be replaced by a spreadsheet.

I should know. I had spent enough time in this office.

"Of course you wouldn't," I said to Mark.

"The thing is," he said, raising his gaze from the Army brochure and looking at me with soulful brown eyes. "I mean, it isn't like we weren't having problems. Every couple has problems. But we were working them out. We were totally working them out."

I'll say. At least if what Claire Lippman had told me was any indication. He and Amber had been the Make-out King and Queen of that little barbecue, anyway.

"And then, for this to happen . . ." He let his gaze drift away from me, toward the clock on the wall behind me. "Especially when everything else was going so great. You know, we have a real shot at the state championship this year. I just . . ."

I swear, as I was sitting there, looking at him, I noticed an unnatural glimmer in his eyes. At first I thought it was just a trick of the flourescent lights overhead. And then it hit me.

Mark Leskowski was crying. Crying. Mark Leskowski. A football player. Crying because he missed his dead girlfriend.

"And there are going to be scouts, you know, from all the major universities," he said, with a barely suppressed sob. "Checking me out.

Checking *me* out. I have a solid chance at getting out of this Podunk town, of going all the way."

Or maybe it was because his football scholarship was going down the drain. Whatever the reason, Mark was *crying*.

I flung a startled glance in the secretary's direction, because I did not know what to do. I mean, I have never dealt with crying football players before. Suicidal brothers, sure. Homicidal maniacs who wanted to kill me, easy. But crying football players?

The secretary was no longer pretending to be absorbed in her game of Minesweeper. She, too, had noticed Mark's tears. And she, too, looked as if she did not know what to do. Her startled gaze met mine, and she shrugged in bewilderment. Then, as if she'd had an idea, she jumped and waved a box of Kleenex at me.

Oh, great. Some help.

Still, there didn't seem to be anything else I could do. I got up and took the Kleenex box from her, then went and sat down beside Mark, and offered it to him.

"Here," I said, laying one hand on his shoulder. "It's okay."

Mark took a handful of Kleenex and pressed them to his eyes. He was swearing softly beneath his breath.

"It's *not* okay," he said vehemently, into the Kleenex. "This is unacceptable. All of this is *unacceptable.*"

"I know," I said, patting his shoulder. It felt

strong and muscular beneath my fingers. "But really, it will all work out. Everything is going to be okay."

It was at that moment that the door to Mr. Goodhart's office swung open, and Special Agents Johnson and Smith came out. They looked down at Mark and me curiously, then seemed to realize what was happening. When they did, both their faces grew hard.

"Mark," Special Agent Smith said, in a voice that I did not think was very friendly, as she took a step toward us. "Would you please come with me?"

When she reached the couch, she bent down and slipped a hand beneath Mark's arm. He rose without protest, keeping the Kleenex to his eyes. Then he let her lead him away, toward one of the conference rooms down the hall.

Special Agent Johnson stood looking down at me, his arms folded across his chest.

"Jessica," he said. "Don't even think about going there."

"What?" I spread my hands out in the universal gesture for innocence. "I didn't say anything."

"But you were about to. Jessica, I'm telling you now, leave this one alone. Unless you know something—"

"Which I don't," I said.

"Then stay out of it. A young woman is dead. I don't want you to be next."

Whoa. Okay, Officer Friendly.

As if realizing how unctuous he'd sounded,

Special Agent Johnson changed the subject. "I'm still anxious to hear"—he unfolded his arms— "about this girl in San Francisco."

"There is no girl in San Francisco," I protested. "Really. I swear."

Special Agent Johnson nodded. "Right. Okay. If that's the way you want it. Read my lips then, Jess. Stay out of this one. Way out."

Then he turned around and followed his partner and Mark.

I looked at the secretary. She looked back at me. Our looks said it all. No way was Mark Leskowski, a boy unafraid to cry in public about his dead girlfriend, a murderer.

"Jessica." Mr. Goodhart came out of his office and looked surprised to see me still sitting there, waiting for him. "Go home."

Go home? Was he nuts? I had just sunk my fist into another student's face. And he was just letting me go home?

"But . . ."

"Go." Mr. Goodhart turned to the secretary. "Get Sheriff Hawkins on the line for me, will you, Helen?"

Go? That was it? Just *go?* I thought I had one more strike, and then I Was Out? Where was the anger-management lecture? Where were the sighs, the "Oh, Jess, I just don't know what I'm going to do with you"s? Where was my week-long detention? That was it? I could just . . . go?

Helen, noticing that I was still sitting there, put her hand over the phone receiver so whoever she was calling wouldn't hear her when she hissed to me, "Jess. What are you waiting for? Go, before he remembers."

I didn't waste any more time after that. I went.

I was sitting on the hood of Ruth's Cabriolet when she came out of the assembly, looking vaguely harassed.

"Oh, hey," she said in surprise when she saw me. "What are you doing here? I thought Mulder and Scully were on your case again."

"It wasn't me they were after this time," I said. I still couldn't keep the wonder out of my voice. The whole thing had just been so bizarre.

"Really?" Ruth unlocked the door to the driver's side and climbed into her car. "What did they want, then?"

"Mark," I said.

"Leskowski?" Ruth looked shocked as she leaned over to unlock the door to my side. "Oh, my God. They must really think he did it."

"Yeah, only he didn't." I opened the door and slid in. "Ruth, you should have seen him. Mark, I mean. I was sitting next to him, you know, outside of Mr. Goodhart's office, and he . . . he was crying."

"Crying?" Ruth turned away from her examination of her lips in the rearview mirror. "He was not."

I assured her that he had been. "It was so sweet," I went on. "I mean, you could tell. He really, really loved her. He feels so bad."

Ruth still looked shocked. "Mark Leskowski. Crying. Who would have thought it?"

"I know. So how did the rest of the memorial service go?"

Ruth described it as she drove us home. Apparently, after the interpretive dance, there'd been a long lecture from a grief counselor the school had hired to help us through this trying time, followed by a moment of silent reflection in which we were all to remember what we had loved about Amber. Then the cheerleaders announced that, directly after school, they were heading back up to Pike's Quarry, to throw flowers into the water as a tribute to Amber. Anyone whose heart had ever been touched by Amber was invited to come along to watch.

"Yeah," Ruth said. "Anyone whose heart was ever touched by Amber was invited. You know what that means."

"Right," I said. "In Crowd Only. You're not going, right?"

"Are you kidding me? Perhaps I didn't make it clear. This particular soiree is being hosted by the Ernie Pyle High School varsity cheerleading squad. In other words, 'fat girls, stay home.'"

I blinked at her, a little taken aback at the vehemence in her tone.

"Ruth," I said. "You're not—"

"Once a fat girl," Ruth said, "always a fat girl. In their eyes, anyway."

"But how you look is not important," I said. "It's what's inside that—"

"Spare me," Ruth said. "Besides, I have chair auditions tomorrow. I have to practice."

I eyed her. Ruth was hard to figure out sometimes. She was so supremely confident about some things—academic stuff, and not chasing boys—but so insecure about others. She really was one of those enigmas wrapped in a mystery people are always talking about. Especially since the same way Ruth claimed cheerleaders felt about fat girls, she felt about Grits.

"I mean, I'm sorry she's dead and all," Ruth went on, "but I highly doubt they'd ever hold an all-school memorial service for you or me, you know, if either of us happened to croak."

"Well," I said. "She did die kind of tragically."

Ruth said a bad word as she turned down Lumley Lane. "Please. She was a cheerleader, all right? Doesn't that about say it all? They don't hold all-school assemblies in the memory of dead cellists or flutists. Just cheerleaders. Hey." Pulling into my driveway, Ruth gaped at me. "Wait a minute. We drove right by Pike's Creek Road, and you didn't say a word. What gives? Don't tell me Mark Leskowski's big baby-blues have replaced the memory of the Jerk's."

"Mark's eyes," I said, with some annoyance, "happen to be brown. And Rob is not a jerk. And I happen to think you're right. Chasing Rob is not the way to get him."

"Uh-huh." Ruth shook her head. "Skip mentioned he gave you and Claire a lift from the bus stop this morning. You talked him into stopping for crullers, didn't you?"

"I didn't talk him into doing anything," I said

indignantly. "He stopped of his own volition."

"Oh, please." Ruth rolled her eyes. "Well? Did you see him?"

"Did I see who?" I asked, stalling for time.

"You know who. The Jerk."

I sighed. "I saw him."

"And?"

"And what? I saw him. He didn't see me. End of story."

"God." Ruth laughed. "You are a piece of work. Hey. What's that?"

I looked down at myself, since that's where she was pointing. "What's what?"

"That. That red spot on your shoe."

I lifted my foot, examining a minuscule drop of red on my beige espadrille.

"Oh," I said. "That's just some of Karen Sue Hankey's blood."

"Her blood?" Ruth looked flabbergasted. "Oh, my God. What did you do to her?"

"Punched her in the face," I said, still feeling a little smug at the memory. "You should have seen it, Ruth. It was beautiful."

"Beautiful?" Ruth banged her head against the steering wheel a few times. "Oh, God. And you were doing so well."

I couldn't understand her dismay.

"Ruth," I said. "She fully deserved it."

"That's no excuse," Ruth said, raising her head. "There's only one justification for hitting someone, Jess, and that's if they try to hit you first, and you swing back in self-defense. You can't just go around *hitting* people all the time, just because you don't like what they say to you. You're going to get into serious trouble."

"I am not," I said. "Not this time. I totally got caught, and Mr. Goodhart didn't even say anything. He just told me to go home."

"Yeah," Ruth said. "Because there was a suspected murderer in his office! He was probably just a little distracted."

"Mark Leskowski," I said, "is not a murderer. What's more, he thoroughly supported my breaking Karen Sue's face. He says she's a wannabe."

"Oh, God," Ruth said. "Why was I cursed with such a screwed-up best friend?"

Since I had just been thinking the same nice thing about her, I did not take offense.

"Let's practice together," I said, "at nine. Okay?" Since we live next door to one another, we frequently open our living room windows and play at the same time, giving the neighborhood a free concert, while also getting in some valuable practice time.

"Okay," Ruth said. "But if you think you can just pop Karen Sue Hankey in the face and never hear about it again, you're the one with another think coming, girlfriend."

I laughed as I hurried up the steps to my house. As if! Karen Sue would probably be so afraid of me from now on, I'd never have to put up with her noxious taunting again. As an added bonus, she probably wasn't going to play so well during her chair audition on Thursday, on account of her swollen nose.

It was with these delicious thoughts that I slipped into the house. I had set only one foot on the stairs leading up to my room when my mother's voice, not sounding too pleased, reached me from the kitchen.

Meekly, I made my way to the back of the house.

"Hi, Mom," I said when I saw her at the kitchen table. To my surprise, my dad was there, too.

But my dad never got home before six on a Tuesday.

"Hey, Dad," I said, noting that neither one of them looked particularly happy. Then my heart started to thump uncomfortably.

"What's the matter?" I asked quickly. "Is Douglas—"

"Douglas," my mother said, her voice so hard it was like ice, "is fine."

"Oh." I looked at the two of them. "It isn't—"

"Michael," my mother said, in that same hard voice, "is also fine."

Relief coursed through me. Well, if it wasn't Douglas, and it wasn't Mike, it couldn't be too bad. Maybe it was even something good. You know, something my parents would think was bad, but I might think was good. Like Great-aunt Rose having dropped dead from a heart attack, for instance.

"So," I said, preparing to look sad. "What's up?"

"We got a call a little while ago," my father said, looking grim.

"You'll never guess who it was," said my mother.

"I give up," I said, thinking, Wow, Great-aunt Rose really *is* dead. "Who was it?"

"Mrs. Hankey," my mother said. "Karen Sue's mother."

Oops.

CHAPTER

7

Busted.

I was so busted.

But you know, I really don't think they had any right to be so mad, seeing as how I was defending the family honor and all.

And what a whiny baby, that Karen Sue, ratting me out to her mother. Of course, in Karen Sue's version of the events leading up to my punching her in the face, she hadn't said any of the things we both know she'd really said. In Karen Sue's version of how it all happened, I was trying to sneak out of assembly, and she tried to stop me—for my own good, of course, and because my leaving early was besmirching Amber Mackey's memory—and I hit her for her efforts.

The whole part about how my denying my psychic powers was what making Douglas sick? Yeah, Karen Sue left that part out.

Oh, and the part about how Douglas doesn't attend church or pray often enough? Yeah, left that part out, too.

My mom didn't believe me when I told her about that part. See, Karen Sue has my mom snowed, just like she's got her own mother snowed. All my mom sees when she looks at Karen Sue is the daughter she always wished she had. You know, the sweet compliant daughter who enters her homemade cookies in the county fair bake-off every year, and puts her hair in curlers at night so the ends will flip just the right way in the morning. My mom never counted on having a daughter like me, who is saving up for a Harley and has her hair cut as short as she possibly can so she won't have to mess with it.

And oh, yeah, who gets into fights all the time, and is in love with a guy who is on probation.

My poor mom.

My dad believed me. The part about what Karen Sue said and all. My mom, like I said before, didn't.

I heard them arguing about it after I was banished to my room, to Think About What I Had Done. I was also supposed to think about how I was going to pay back Karen Sue's medical bill (two hundred and forty nine dollars for a trip to the emergency room. She didn't even have to get stitches). Mrs. Hankey was also threatening to sue me for the mental anguish I'd inflicted on her daughter. Karen Sue's mental anguish, according to her mother, was worth about five thousand dollars. I didn't have five thousand dollars. I only had about a thousand dollars left in my bank account, after my Michigan City outlet store shopping spree.

I was supposed to sit in my room and think about how I was going to raise another four thousand, two hundred and forty-nine dollars.

Instead, I went into Douglas's room to see what he was doing.

"Hey, loser," I started to say as I barged in, as is my tradition where Douglas is concerned. "Guess what happened to me to—"

Only I didn't finish, because Douglas wasn't there.

Yeah, that's right. He wasn't in his room. About eight million comic books were lying around his bed, but no Douglas.

Which was kind of weird. Because Douglas, ever since he got sent home from State College for trying to kill himself, never went anywhere. Seriously. He just sat in his room, reading.

Oh, sure, sometimes Dad forced him to go to one of the restaurants and bus tables or whatever, but except for that and when he was at his shrink's office, Douglas was always in his room.

Always.

Maybe, I decided, he'd run out of comic books and gone downtown to get more. That made sense. Because the few times he had strayed from his room in the past six months, that's where he'd gone.

It was no fun sitting in my room, thinking

about what I'd done. For one thing, I didn't think what I'd done was so bad. For another, it was August, so it was still pretty nice out, for late afternoon. I sat in the dormer window and gazed down at the street. My room is on the third floor of our house—in the attic, actually, which is the former servants' quarters. Our house is the oldest one on Lumley Lane, built around the turn of the century. The *twentieth* century. The city even came and put a plaque on it (the house, I mean), saying it was a historic landmark.

From the third floor dormer windows—my bedroom windows—you could see all up and down Lumley Lane. For once there was no white van parked across the street, monitoring my activities. That's because Special Agents Johnson and Smith were back at the school with Mark Leskowski.

Poor Mark. I had no way of knowing how he must be feeling—I mean, if Rob ever turned up dead, God only knew what I'd do, and we'd never even gone out. Well, for more than like five minutes, anyway. And if I got blamed for having done it—you know, killing him—I'd flip out for true.

Still, it looked as if Mark was everyone's lead suspect. His parents had, as Ruth had predicted, hired Mr. Abramowitz as their son's attorney—not that he'd been officially charged with the murder, but it certainly looked as if he would be.

The way I found this out was, my parents yelled up the stairs to me that they were going next door to consult with Ruth's dad about Karen Sue's case against me. Mr. Abramowitz had apparently just got home from a consult he'd been doing over at Ernie Pyle. What else could he have been consulting about over there? The new mascot uniform?

"There's some leftover ziti in the fridge," my mom hollered up the stairs to me. "Heat it up if you get hungry. Did you hear that, Douglas?"

Which was when I realized my mom didn't know Douglas was gone.

"I'll tell him," I called to her. Which wasn't a lie. I *would* tell him. When he got home.

You wouldn't think it was a big deal, a twenty-year-old guy going out for a while. But really, for Douglas, it was. A big deal, I mean. Mom was totally spastic about him, thinking he was like this delicate flower that would wilt at the slightest exposure to the elements.

Which was such a joke, really, because Douglas was no flower. He was just, you know, figuring things out. Like the rest of us.

Only he was being a little more cautious than the rest of us.

"And don't you," my mother yelled up the stairs, "even think about going anywhere, Jessica. When your father and I get home, the three of us are going to sit down for a nice long *chat*."

Well. That certainly didn't sound like Dad had convinced her I'd been telling the truth about what Karen Sue had said. Yet, anyway.

From my dormer window, I watched them leave. They crossed our front lawn, then cut through the hedge that separated our property from the Abramowitzes', even though they were always telling me to take the long way, or the hedge would suffer permanent root damage. Whatever. I got up from the window and went downstairs to see what was up with the ziti.

I had just opened the fridge when someone turned the crank to our doorbell. Because our house is so old, it has this antique doorbell with a handle you have to turn, not a button you push.

"Coming," I called, wondering who it could be. Ruth would never ring the doorbell. She'd just walk right in. And everyone else we knew would call first before coming over.

When I got into the foyer, I saw what definitely appeared to be a masculine shape behind the lace curtain that covered the window in the front door. It looked to be about the right size and shape for Rob.

My heart, ridiculously, skipped a beat, even though I knew perfectly well Rob would never just walk up to my front door and ring the bell. Not since I told him how much it would freak out my mom if she ever found out I liked a guy who a) wasn't college-bound and b) had spent time in the Big House.

Maybe, I thought, for one panic-stricken moment, Rob *did* see me in the back of Skip's Trans Am, and he was coming over to ask me if I was completely out of my mind, going around, spying on him like that.

But when I flung open the door, I saw that it wasn't Rob at all. My heart didn't stop its crazy gymnastics, though.

Because instead of Rob Wilkins standing on my front porch, it was Mark Leskowski.

"Hey," he said when he saw me. His smile was nervous and shy and wonderful, all at the same time. "Whew. I'm glad it was you. You know. Who answered the door. All of a sudden I was like, 'Whoa, what if her dad answers.' But it's you."

I just stood there and stared. You would have, too, if you'd opened up your front door and found your school's star quarterback standing there, smiling shyly.

"Um," Mark said, when I didn't say anything right away. "Can I, um, talk to you? Just for a few minutes?"

I looked behind me. There was no one in the house, of course. Looking behind me had been pure reflex.

The thing was, even though I'd never had a boy come over to my house to visit me before, I was pretty sure my parents wouldn't like it if I invited him in when they weren't home.

Mark must have realized what I was thinking, since he said, "Oh, I don't have to come in. We could sit out here, if you want."

I shook my head. I was still feeling a little dazed. It is not every day you open up your door and see a guy like Mark Leskowski standing on your porch.

I guess it was on account of this dazed feeling that I opened up my mouth and blurted, "Why aren't you at the memorial service?"

Mark didn't seem offended by my bluntness, however. He looked down at his feet and murmured, "I couldn't. I mean, the one today at school was bad enough. But to go back there, where it happened . . . I just couldn't."

Oh, God. My heart lurched for him. The guy was clearly hurting.

"The only time since all of this started that I've felt even semi-human was when I was talking to you," Mark said, lifting his gaze to meet mine. "I was hoping we could . . . you know. Talk some more. If you haven't eaten, I was thinking maybe we could go grab something. To eat, I mean. Nothing fancy or anything. Maybe just pizza."

Pizza. Mark Leskowski wanted to take me out for pizza.

I said, "Sure," and closed the front door behind me. "Pizza's fine."

Yeah, I know, okay? I know my mother said not to leave the house. I know I was being punished for trying to deviate Karen Sue Hankey's septum.

But look, Mark needed me, all right? You could *see* the need right there in his face.

And seriously, who else was he going to turn to? Who else but me had ever been in anything like the kind of trouble he was in? I mean, I knew what it was like to be hunted, like an animal, by the so-called authorities. I knew what it was like to have everyone, everyone in the whole world against you.

And yeah, okay, no one had ever suspected me of committing murder. But hadn't everyone at school been going around blaming me for Amber's death? Wasn't that almost the same thing?

So I went with him. I got into his car—a black BMW. It so totally figured—and we drove downtown, and no, I never once thought, *Gee, I hope he doesn't drive out into the woods and try to kill me.*

This is because, for one thing, I didn't believe Mark Leskowski was capable of killing anyone, on account of his being so sensitive and all. And for another thing, it was broad daylight. No one tries to kill someone else in broad daylight.

Furthermore, even though I am only five foot tall, I have bested bigger guys than Mark Leskowski. As Douglas is fond of pointing out, I feel no compunction whatsoever against fighting dirty if I have to.

Can I just tell you that the world looks different from the inside of a BMW? Or maybe it is just that it looks different from the inside of Mark Leskowski's BMW. His BMW has tinted windows, so everything looks kind of . . . *better* from inside his car.

Except for Mark, of course. He, I was discovering, always looks good.

Especially when, like now, he was worried. His dark eyebrows kind of furrowed together in this adorably vulnerable way . . . kind of like a golden retriever puppy that wasn't sure where it had put its ball.

"It's just that they all think I did it," he said as we started down Lumley Lane. "And I . . .I just can't believe it. I mean, that they'd think that. I loved Amber."

I murmured something encouraging. All I could think was, *Heather Montrose*, please *be downtown when we get there.* Please *see me getting out of Mark Leskowski's BMW.* Please *see me eating pizza with him.* Please.

It was wrong of me—so wrong—to want to be seen in the BMW of a boy whose girlfriend had, just days before, died tragically.

On the other hand, it was wrong of Heather—so wrong—to have been so mean to me about something that was in no way my fault.

"But these Feds . . . ," Mark went on. "Well, you know them. Right? I mean, they seem to know you. They're just so . . . secretive. It's like they know something. Like they have some kind of proof I did it."

"Oh," I said as we turned onto Second Street. "I'm sure they don't."

"Of course they don't," Mark said. "Because I didn't do it."

"Right," I said. Too bad I didn't have a cell phone. Because then I could make up some excuse about how I had to call Ruth, and then I could tell her I was with Mark. Mark *Leskowski*. That I was with *Mark Leskowski* in his *BMW*.

Why does every sixteen-year-old girl in the entire world have a cell phone but me?

"That's right," Mark said. "They don't. Because if they did, they'd have arrested me already. Right?"

I looked at him. Beautiful. So beautiful. No Rob Wilkins, of course. But a hottie, just the same.

"Right," I said.

"And they'd have told you. Wouldn't they? I mean, wouldn't they have told you? If they had something on me?"

"Of course they wouldn't have told me," I said. "Why would they have told me? What do you think I am, some kind of narc?"

"Of course not," Mark said. "It's just that you seem to be, you know, real friendly with one another. . . ."

I let out a bark of laughter at that.

"Sorry to disappoint you, Mark," I said. "But Special Agents Johnson and Smith and I are not exactly friends. Basically, I have something they want, and that's about it."

Mark glanced at me curiously. We were stopped at an intersection, so it was okay that he was looking at me and not at the road, but I'd noticed that Mark also had a tendency to stare at me when he should have been paying attention to where we were going. This, in addition to his seeming to think that stop signs were mere suggestions, and that it wasn't in the least bit necessary to maintain a distance of at least two car lengths from the vehicle in front of him, led me to believe Mark wasn't the world's best driver.

"What," he asked me, "do you have that they want?"

I looked back at him, but my look wasn't curious. I was amazed. How could he not know? How could he not have heard? It had been all over the local papers for weeks, and most of the national papers for about the same amount of time. It had been on the news, and there'd even been some talk about making a movie out of the whole thing, except of course I wasn't too enthused about seeing my personal life transferred to the big screen.

"Hello," I said. "Lightning Girl. Remember?"

"Oh," he said. "That whole psychic thing. Yeah. Right."

But that wasn't the only thing Mark had forgotten about. I figured that out when he swung his car into the parking lot for Mastriani's. Mastriani's is one of my family's restaurants. It is the fanciest of the three, though it does indeed serve pizza. I thought it was a little weird that Mark was taking me to my own family's restaurant, but I figured, well, it *is* the best pizza in town, so why complain?

It wasn't until we'd walked through the door—Heather Montrose had not, unfortunately, been downtown to see me get out of Mark Leskowski's BMW—and the waitress who had been assigned to show us to our table went, "Why, Jessica. Hello," that I realized what a huge, colossal mistake I had just made.

Because of course Mark wasn't the only one forgetting things. I'd forgotten that the new waitress my dad had just hired for Mastriani's was none other than Rob's mom.

CHAPTER

8

Yeah. That's right. Rob's mom.

Not that my dad knew she was Rob's mom, of course. I mean, he might have known she had a kid and all, but he didn't know that I was sort of seeing that kid.

Well, all right, that I was madly in love with that kid.

No, my dad had hired Mrs. Wilkins because she'd been out of work after losing her job when the local plastics factory closed down, and I'd told him about her, saying she was a real nice lady and all. I never said how I knew her, though. I never went, Hey, Dad, you should hire the mother of the guy I am madly in love with, even though he won't go out with me because he considers me jailbait and he's eighteen and on probation.

Yeah. I didn't say that.

But of course up until the moment I saw Mrs. Wilkins standing there with a couple of menus in her hand, I totally forgot she worked at Mastriani's . . . that she had been working there most of the summer while I'd been away at camp, and had been doing, from what I'd heard, a real good job.

And now she was going to get to wait on me— the girl who might, if she played her cards right, one day be her daughter-in-law—while I ate pizza with the Ernie Pyle High quarterback who, by the way, appeared to be a suspect in his girl-friend's murder.

Great. Just great. I tell you, with that, in addition to Skip's apparent crush on me, everyone thinking I was responsible for Amber turning up dead, and Karen Sue Hankey's lawsuit against me, my school year was shaping up nicely, thank you.

"Hi, Mrs. Wilkins," I said, with a smile so forced, I thought my cheeks would break. "How are you?"

"Well, I'm just fine, thanks," Mrs. Wilkins said. She was a pretty lady with a lot of red hair piled up on her head with a tortoiseshell clip. "It's great to see you. I heard you were away at music camp."

"Um, yes, ma'am," I said. "Working as a counselor. I got back a couple of days ago."

And your son still hasn't called me. Three days, three days I've been back in town, and has he so much as even driven past my house on his Indian?

No. Nothing. Nada. Zilch.

"That must have been fun," Mrs. Wilkins said.

It was right then that I saw, with horror, that she was leading us to Table Seven, the "make-out" table in the darkest corner of the dining room.

No! I wanted to scream. Not the make-out table, Mrs. Wilkins! This isn't a date, I swear it! This . . . is . . . not . . . a . . . date!

"Here you go," Mrs. Wilkins said, putting the menus down on top of Table Seven. "Now you all have a seat and I'll be right with you with some ice waters. Unless you'd prefer Cokes?"

"Coke sounds good to me," Mark said.

"I'll . . . I'll just have water," I managed to choke. The make-out table! Oh, God, not the make-out table!

"Coke and a water it is, then," Mrs. Wilkins said, and then she bustled away.

Great. Just great. I knew what was going to happen now, of course. Mrs. Wilkins was going to tell Rob that she'd seen me, on a date, with Mark Leskowski. She might even tell him about the make-out table.

Then Rob was going to think I'd finally accepted his mandate that we not see each other romantically. And what was going to happen after that? I'll tell you: He was going to start thinking it'd be okay for him to go out with one of those floozies from Chick's Biker Bar, where he hangs out sometimes. How am I supposed to compete with a twenty-seven year old named

Darla with tattoos and her own hog? I can't, I tell you. Not with an eleven o'clock curfew.

My life was over. So over.

"Hey," Mark said, lowering his menu. In the candlelight—yes, there was candlelight. Come on. It was the make-out table—he looked more handsome than ever. But what did it matter? What did it matter, how handsome Mark was? Mark wasn't the one I wanted.

"I forgot," Mark said. "You own this place, or something, don't you?"

"Something like that," I said, not even attempting to hide my misery.

"Whoa," Mark said. "I'm sorry. I mean, I don't want you to think I picked this place so I wouldn't have to pay or anything. I just really like Mastriani pizza." He put the menu down. "But we can totally go somewhere else, if you want to—"

"Oh, yeah? Where, exactly?" I asked.

"Well," he said. "There's Joe's. . . ."

"We own Joe's, too," I said with a sigh.

"Oh." Mark winced. "That means you probably own Joe Junior's, too, then, huh?"

"Yeah," I said. I lifted my chin. Okay. It was the make-out table. But that didn't mean I had to make out with Mark Leskowski. Not that that would be such a sacrifice and all, but, under the circumstances, it would hardly be appropriate.

"Look, it's all right," I said, trying to rally my downtrodden spirits. "We can stay. You just have to tip really good, okay? Because I . . . know this waitress. Really well."

"No problem," Mark said, and then he started asking me what I liked on my pizza.

Look, despite all the evidence to the contrary, I'm not the world's biggest dope. I knew why Mark had asked me out, and it wasn't because since I'd started wearing miniskirts to school he'd suddenly realized what a great pair of legs I've got. It wasn't even because in the guidance office earlier that day we'd had that lovely little bonding moment, before the Feds so rudely busted in on us.

No, Mark had asked me out because he thought he could pump me for information . . . information I didn't have. Did Special Agents Johnson and Smith suspect him of murdering his girlfriend? Maybe.

Or maybe they'd just wanted to ask him some questions, so they could figure out who else might possibly have done it.

And hadn't I wanted to do the exact same thing? Pump him for information, I mean, about Amber's last moments on earth . . . or at least her last moments with Mark? Because however strenuously I tried to deny that Amber's death was my fault, there was still a part of me that felt like, if I'd only been around, it wouldn't have happened. I was convinced that if Heather and those guys had managed to reach me, I'd have been able to find Amber before she was killed. I knew it. I knew it the way I knew that when Kurt, the head chef at Mastriani's, found out I was sitting at Table Seven, he'd arrange the pepperonis on my pizza in the shape of a heart. Which he did, to my utter mortification.

Mark hardly even noticed. That's how strung out he was about the whole being-suspected-of-his-girlfriend's-murder thing. He just handed me a slice, and, as we ate, we talked about how it felt to be grilled by the FBI.

And the sad part was, that was about all we had in common. The both of us having been interrogated by the FBI, I mean. That, and our mutual dislike of Karen Sue Hankey. Mark's whole life, it appeared, was about football. He was being scouted, he explained, by the coaches at several Big Ten schools, and even a couple out east. He was going to take the best scholarship he could get, and play college ball until the NFL came knocking.

This seemed like a reasonable plan to me, except that even I, a football ignoramus, knew that the NFL did not come knocking on the door of every college player. What if, I asked, that plan fell through? What was his backup plan? Medical school? Law school? What?

Mark stared at me blankly over our pepperoni with extra cheese. "Backup plan?" he echoed. "There's no backup plan."

I thought maybe I hadn't expressed my meaning with sufficient clarity.

"No," I said. "Really. Like what if you don't make it to the pros? Then what?"

Mark shook his head, but more like he was flicking away something unpleasant that had landed on his head than actually disagreeing with me.

"Failure," he said, "is unacceptable."

There it was again. The whole unacceptable thing he'd mentioned back in the guidance office. These athletes, I couldn't help noting, really took their calling seriously.

"Unacceptable?" I coughed. "Yeah, okay. Failure is unacceptable, of course. But sometimes it happens. And then . . . well, you have to accept it."

Mark regarded me calmly from across the table.

"That's a common mistake," he said. "Many people actually believe that. But not me. That's what makes me different than everybody else, Jess. Because to me, failure is simply not an option."

Oh. Well. Okay.

It was kind of weird, I have to say, being out with Amber Mackey's boyfriend. Not just the fact that we were being waited on by the mother of the guy I really liked, either. No, it was the whole Amber-Was-Here thing. I couldn't help thinking, What had Amber seen in this guy? Yeah, he was totally buff, but he was also kind of . . . boring. I mean, he didn't know anything about music, or motorcycles, or anything fun like that. He'd seen most of the latest movies, but the ones I thought were good, he hadn't liked, and the one he'd liked, I'd thought were stupid beyond belief. And he didn't have time for anything else, like reading books or watching

TV, because he was always at football practice.

Seriously. Not even comic books. Not even the WWF.

Not that Amber had been Ms. Intellectual herself. But she at least had had interests beyond cheerleading. I mean, she'd always been organizing bake sales for some charity or another. It seemed like every week she had a new cause, from collecting baby things for unwed mothers to holding food drives for starving people in African nations none of us had ever even heard of.

But maybe I was being too hard on Mark. I mean, at least he had a goal, right? A lot of guys don't. My brother Douglas, for instance. Well, I guess his goal is to get better. But what is he going to do when he's accomplished that?

Rob has a goal. He wants to have a motorcycle repair shop of his own. Until he's saved up enough money for it, he's going to work in his uncle's garage.

You know who doesn't have a goal? Yeah, that'd be me. No goal. I mean, beyond keeping the Federal Bureau of Investigation from finding out I'm still psychic. Oh, and getting a Harley when I turn eighteen. And one day being Mrs. Robert Wilkins.

But I have to have a career first. Before I can get married, I mean. And I don't even know what kind I want. You know, career-wise. I mean, you can't make a living finding missing kids. Well, you probably could, but I wouldn't want to. You can't take money for doing something any decent human being should do for free. I'd attended church often enough to know *that*, at least.

So I told myself to stop being so critical of Mark. The guy was going through a hard time.

And he did leave a really nice tip for Mrs. Wilkins, so that was all right.

As we were on our way out, she waved at us and said, "Y'all have fun now."

Y'all have fun now. My heart lurched. I did not want to have fun. Not with Mark Leskowski. The only person I wanted to have fun with was Rob Wilkins. Your son Rob, okay, Mrs. Wilkins? He's the only person I want to have fun with. So would you please do me a favor and DON'T tell him you saw me here tonight with Mark Leskowski? Please? Would you do that for me?

And for Pete's sake, whatever else you do, DON'T tell him about the make-out table. For the love of God, don't mention the make-out table.

Only of course I couldn't say that to her. I mean, how could I say that to her?

So instead all I did was wave back at her, feeling sick to my stomach, and say, "Thank you!"

Oh, God. I was so dead.

I tried not to think about it. I tried to be all bright and chipper, like Amber had always been. Seriously. No matter how early in the morning it was, or how foul the weather outside, Amber had always been cheerful in homeroom. Amber had really liked school. Amber had been one of those people who'd woken up every day and gone, Good morning, Sunshine, to herself in the mirror.

At least, she'd always seemed that way to me.

Of course, a fat lot of good it had done her, in the end.

I tried not to think about this as Mark walked me back to his car. I tried to keep my mind on happier subjects.

The only problem was, I couldn't think of any. Happy things, I mean.

"I guess you probably have to be getting home," Mark said as he opened the passenger door for me.

"Yeah," I said. "I mean, I'm sort of in trouble. For the whole Karen Sue Hankey thing, I mean."

"Okay," Mark said. "But do you want to maybe stop at the Moose for a minute? For a shake or something?"

The Moose. The Chocolate Moose. That was the ice-cream stand across from the movie house on Main where all the popular kids hung out. Seriously. Ruth and I hadn't been to the Moose since we were little kids because as soon as we'd hit puberty, we'd realized only the beautiful people from school were allowed to go there. If you weren't a jock or a cheerleader and you showed up at the Moose, everybody there gave you dirty looks.

Which was actually okay, because the ice cream there wasn't as good as it was at the Thirty-one Flavors down the street. Still, the idea of going to the Moose with Mark Leskowski . . .

well, it was strange and off-putting and thrilling, all at the same time.

"Sure," I said, casually as if boys asked me to go to the Moose with them every day of the week. "A shake'd be good, I guess."

There weren't many people hanging out at the Moose at first. Just Mark and me, and a couple of Wrestlerettes, who gave me the evil eye when I first walked up. But when they saw I was with Mark Leskowski, they relaxed, and even smiled. Todd Mintz was there with a couple of his friends. He grunted a hello to me and high-fived Mark.

I had a mint-chocolate-chip blizzard. Mark had something with Heath candy bar crunches sprinkled in. We sat on top of a picnic table that had a view all the way up Main Street, right up to the courthouse. The courthouse and, I couldn't help noticing, the jail. Behind the jail, the sun was setting in all these vibrant colors. It was beautiful and all—a true Indian summer sunset. But it was still, you know. The *jail*.

The jail where Mark might end up, admiring the sunset from behind bars.

I think he sort of realized that, too, because he turned away from the sunset and started asking me about my classes. That's desperation for you, when you start asking someone about their classes. I mean, if I hadn't realized before then that Mark and I had nothing in common, that would have been a real big clue.

Fortunately, a car pulled up about midway

through my description of my U.S. Government class, and the people who piled out of it all started calling out Mark's name.

Only it wasn't, as I'd first thought, because they were so glad to see him. It was because they had something to tell him.

"Oh, my God." It was Tisha Murray, from my homeroom. She still had on her uniform from the memorial service—Tisha was on the varsity cheerleading squad—but she'd apparently left her pompons in the car.

"Oh, God, I'm so glad we found you," she gushed. "We were looking everywhere. Look, you've got to come quick. It's an emergency!"

Mark slid off the picnic table, his shake forgotten.

"What?" he asked, reaching out to take Tisha by either shoulder. "What's happened? What do you need me to do?"

"Not *you*," Tisha said, rudely. Except I don't think she meant to be rude. She was just too hysterical to remember social niceties. "*Her*."

She pointed. At me.

"You," Tisha said to me. "We need you."

"*Me?*" I nearly fell off the picnic table. Never before had a member of the Ernie Pyle varsity cheerleading squad expressed even the slightest interest in me. Well, except for the past two days, when they'd been berating me for letting Amber die. "What do you need *me* for?"

"Because it's happened again!" Tisha said. "Only this time it's Heather. He's got her.

Whoever killed Amber has got Heather now! You've got to find her. Do you hear me? You've got to find her, before he strangles her, too!"

CHAPTER

9

It probably isn't politic to slap a cheerleader. That's exactly what I did, though.

Hey, she was hysterical, all right? Isn't that what you're supposed to do to people who can't get ahold of themselves?

Looking back, though, it probably wasn't the smartest thing to do. Because all it did was reduce Tisha to tears. Not just tears, either, but big baby sobs. Mark had to get the story out of Jeff Day, who didn't know nearly as many words as Tisha did.

"We were at the memorial thingie," he said as Tisha wept in the arms of Vicky Huff, a Pompette. "You know, up at the quarry. The girls threw a bunch of the wreaths and flowers and crap from the service into the water. It was all symbolic and shit."

Have I mentioned that Jeff Day is not exactly on the honor roll?

"And then it was time to go, and everyone went back to their cars . . . everyone except Heather. She was just . . . gone."

"What do you mean," Mark demanded, "by *gone?*"

Jeff shrugged his massive shoulders.

"You know, Mark," he said. "Just . . . just gone."

"That's unacceptable," Mark said.

I wasn't sure what Mark was referring to . . . the fact that Heather had disappeared, or Jeff's shrugging off that disappearance. When, however, Jeff stammered, "What I mean . . . what I mean is, we looked, but we couldn't find her," I realized Mark had meant Jeff's answer. Jeff's hurrying to correct himself reminded me that, as quarterback, Mark was in a position of some authority over these guys.

"People don't do that, Jeff," I said. "People just don't just disappear."

"I know," Jeff said, looking a little miserable. "But Heather did."

"It was just like in that movie," Tisha said, lifting her tear-stained face. "That *Blair Witch* movie, where those kids disappeared in the woods. It was just like that. One second, Heather was there, and the next, she was gone. We called and called for her, and looked everywhere, but it was like . . . like she had vanished. Like that witch had gotten her."

I regarded Tisha with raised eyebrows.

"I highly doubt," I said, "that Heather's disappearance is the result of witchcraft, Tisha."

"No," Tisha said, wiping her eyes with her twig-like fingers. The tiniest member of the varsity squad, Tisha was the one who always ended up on the top of the trophy pyramid, or came popping up into the air, to land in a cradle of arms on the gym floor beneath her. "I know it wasn't really a witch. But it was probably, you know, a Grit."

"A Grit," I said.

"Yeah. I saw this movie once about these Grits who lived in the mountains, and they totally kidnapped Michael J. Fox's wife—you know, that Tracy Pollan. She was an Olympic biathlete, and they kidnapped her and tried to make her, like, tote their water and all. Until she, like, escaped."

I can't believe my life sometimes. I really can't.

"Maybe some freaky Grits like those ones in the movie, who live out in the woods by the quarry, got her. I've seen them out there, you know. They live in shacks, with no running water or electricity, and, like, an outhouse." Tisha started sobbing all over again. "They've probably stuffed her in the bottom of their outhouse!"

I had to give Tisha her propers for having such a colorful imagination. But still, this seemed a bit much to me.

"Let me see if I have this straight," I said. "You think a deranged hillbilly, who lives out by Pike's Quarry, has kidnapped Heather and stuffed her down his toilet."

"I've heard of that kinda thing happening," Jeff Day said.

But instead of supporting his fellow team member, Mark snapped, "That's the stupidest thing I ever heard."

Jeff Day was the kind of guy who, if anybody else had called him stupid, would have slammed his fist into the speaker's face. But not, evidently, if it happened to be Mark Leskowski. Mark, it appeared, was next to godlike in Jeff's book.

"Sorry, dude," he murmured, looking shame-faced.

Mark ignored his teammate.

"Have any of you," he wanted to know, "called the police?"

"Course we did," another player, Roy Hicks, said indignantly, not wanting to look bad, the way his teammate Jeff had, in front of the QB.

"A bunch of sheriff's deputies came up to the quarry," Tisha chimed in, "and they're helping everyone look for her. They even brought some of those sniffer dogs. We only left"—she turned mascara-smudged eyes toward me—"to look for *her.*" Tisha could not seem to remember my name. And why should she? I was so far out of her social sphere as to be invisible. . . .

Except when it came to rescuing her friends from psychotic hillbillies, apparently.

"You've got to find her," Tisha said, her damp eyes aglow with the last rays of the setting sun. "*Please.* Before . . . it's too late."

This blew. I mean it. How was I supposed to convince the Federal Bureau of Investigation that

I don't have psychic powers anymore, when I can't even convince my own peers of it?

"Look, Tisha," I said, aware that not just Tisha was gazing at me hopefully, but also Mark, Jeff Day, Todd Mintz, Roy Hicks, and a veritable Whitman's Sampler of cheerleaders. "I don't . . . I mean, I can't . . ."

"Please," Tisha whispered. "She's my best friend. How would *you* like it if your best friend got kidnapped?"

Damn.

Look, it wasn't like I harbored ill feelings toward Heather Montrose. I did, of course, but that wasn't the point. The point was, I was trying to keep a low profile with the whole psychic thing.

But if Tisha was right, then there was a serial killer loose. He might very well have Heather in his clutches, the same way that, a few days earlier, he'd had Amber in his clutches. Could I really sit around and let a girl—even a girl like Heather Montrose, who, after Karen Sue Hankey, was one of my least favorite people—die?

No. No, I could not.

"I don't have ESP anymore," I said, just so that later on, no one would be able to say I'd agreed to any of this. "But I'll give it a try."

Tisha exhaled gustily, as if she'd been holding her breath until I gave my answer.

"Oh, thank you," she cried. "Thank you!"

"Yeah," I said. "Whatever. But look, I need something of hers."

"Something of whose?" Tisha cocked her head, making her look a lot like a bird. A sparrow, maybe, eyeing a worm.

Yeah. That'd be me. I'd be the worm.

"Something of Heather's," I explained, slowly, so she'd be sure to understand. "Do you have a sweater of hers, or something?"

"I have her pompons," Tisha said, and she bounced back toward the car she'd arrived in.

Todd Mintz looked perplexed. "That's really how you find them?" he asked. "By touching something that belongs to the missing person?"

"Yeah," I said. "Well. Sort of."

It wasn't, of course. Because here's the thing: since that day last spring, when I was hit by lightning, I'd found a lot of people, all right. But I'd only found one of them while I'd been awake. Seriously. Everybody else, it had taken sleep to summon their location to, as Douglas had put it, my mind's eye. That's how my particular psychic ability worked. While I slept.

Which meant that, as a future career option, I was going to have to rule out fortune-telling. You were never going to catch me sitting in a tent with a crystal ball and a big old turban on my head. I could no sooner predict the future than I could fly. All I can do—all I've *ever* been able to do, since the day of that storm—is find missing people.

And I can only do that in my sleep.

Except once. One time, when one of the campers I'd been assigned to watch had run away, I'd hugged his pillow and gotten this weird flash. Really. It was just like a picture inside my head, of exactly where the kid was, and what he was doing.

Whether or not this would happen with the help of Heather's pompons, I had no way of knowing. But I knew that if the same person who'd killed Amber had gotten hold of Heather, we couldn't afford to wait until morning to find her.

"Here." Tisha rushed up to me and shoved two big balls of shimmery silver and white streamers into my hands. "Now find her, quick."

I looked down at the pompons. They were surprisingly heavy. No wonder all the girls on the squad had such cut arm muscles. I'd thought it was from all those cartwheels, but really, it was from hauling these things around.

"Uh, Tisha," I said, aware that every single patron of the Chocolate Moose was looking down at me. "I can't, um . . . I think maybe I need to go home and try it. How about if I come up with anything, I'll call you and let you know?"

Tisha didn't seem particularly enthused by this idea, but what else could I say? I wasn't going to stand there and inhale the scent of Heather Montrose's pompons. (Which was how I'd found Shane. By smelling his pillow, though, not his pompons.)

Fortunately, Mark, at least, seemed to understand, and, taking me by the elbow, said, "I should be getting you home, anyway."

And so, under the watchful gazes of most of Ernie Pyle High's elite, Mark Leskowski escorted me back to his BMW, tucked me gently into the passenger seat, and then got behind the wheel and drove me slowly home.

Slowly not because he didn't want our evening together to end, but because he was so busy talking, I guess it was hard for him to accelerate at the same time.

"You get what this means, don't you?" he asked as we inched down Second Street. "If Heather really is missing—if the same person who killed Amber really has done the same thing to Heather—well, they can't keep on suspecting me, can they? Because I was with you the whole time. Right? I mean, right? Those FBI people can't say I had anything to do with it."

"Right," I said, looking down at Heather's pompons. Was this going to work? I wondered. I mean, would a lapful of pompons really lead me to a missing girl? It didn't seem very likely, but I closed my eyes, dug my fingers into the feathery strands, and tried to concentrate.

"And before I was with you," Mark was saying, "I was with them. Seriously. I came straight to your house from my interview with them. The FBI guys, I mean. So I never had an opportunity to do anything to Heather. She was all the way out at the quarry, with everybody else. And that waitress. She saw me with you, too."

"Right." It was really hard to concentrate, what with Mark talking so much.

Oh, well, I thought. I'll just wait until I get home, and try it there, in the privacy of my own bedroom. I'll have plenty of opportunity, once I get home.

Only of course I didn't. Because my parents had gotten home before I had, and were waiting for me on the front porch, their expressions on the grim side.

Busted again!

Mark, as he pulled into our driveway, went, "Are those your parents?"

"Yes," I said, gulping. I was so dead.

"They look nice." Mark waved at them as he got out of his car and walked around it to open my door. One thing you had to say about Mark Leskowski: he was a gentleman and all.

"Hello, Mr. and Mrs. Mastriani," he called to them. "I hope you don't mind my taking your daughter out for a quick bite to eat. I tried to have her home promptly, as it's a school night."

Whoa. Didn't Mark realize he was laying it on a little thick? I mean, my parents aren't morons.

My mom and dad just sat there—my mom on the porch swing, my dad on the porch steps— and stared as I emerged from Mark's BMW. I had never seen them looking so worried. That was it. I was dead meat.

"Well, it was very nice to meet you, Mr. and Mrs. Mastriani," Mark said. Exercising some of that charm that made him such an effective leader on the ball field, he added, "And may I say that I have enjoyed dining in your restaurants many times? They are particularly fine."

My dad, looking a little astonished, went, "Um, thank you, son."

To me, Mark said, picking up the hand that was not clutching Heather Montrose's pompons, "Thank you, Jessica, for being such a good listener. I really needed that tonight."

He didn't kiss me or anything. He just gave my hand a squeeze, winked, climbed back into his car, and drove away.

Leaving me to face the firing squad alone.

I turned around and squared my shoulders. Really, this was ridiculous. I mean, I am sixteen years old. A grown woman, practically. If I want to punch a girl in the face and then go have a nice dinner with the quarterback of the football team, well, that is my God-given prerogative. . . .

"Mom," I said. "Dad. Listen. I can explain—"

"Jessica," my mother said, getting up from the porch swing. "Where is your brother?"

I blinked at them. The sun had set, and it wasn't easy to see them in the gloom. Still, there wasn't anything wrong with my ears. My mom had just asked me where my brother was. Not where I had been. Where my brother was.

Was it possible that I was not in trouble for going out after all?

"You mean Douglas?" I asked stupidly, because I still could not quite believe my good fortune.

"No," my father said sarcastically. He wasn't worried enough, apparently, to have lost his sense of humor. "Your brother Michael. Of course we mean Douglas. When's the last time you saw him?"

"I don't know," I said. "This morning, I guess."

"Oh, God!" My mother started pacing the length of the porch floor. "I knew it. He's run away. Joe, I'm calling the police."

"He's twenty years old, Toni," my father said. "If he wants to go out, he can go out. There's no law against it."

"But his medicine!" my mom cried. "How do we know he took his medication before he left?"

My dad shrugged. "His doctor says he's been taking it regularly."

"But how do we know he took it *today?*" My mother pulled open the screen door. "That's it. I'm calling the—"

We all heard it at the same time. Whistling. Someone was coming down Lumley Lane, whistling.

I knew who it was at once, of course. Douglas had always been the best whistler in the family. It was he, in fact, who'd taught me to do it. I could still only manage a few folk songs, but Douglas could whistle whole symphony pieces, without even seeming to pause for breath.

When he emerged into the circle of light thrown by the porch lamp, which my mother had hastily turned on, he stopped, and blinked a few times. From one of his hands dangled a bag from the comic book store downtown.

"Hey," he said, looking at us. "What's this? Family meeting? And you started without me?"

My mother just stood there, sputtering. My dad heaved a sigh and got up.

"There," he said to my mother. "You see, Toni? I told you he was all right. Come on, let's go inside. I'm missing the ballgame."

My mother, without a word, turned and went into the house.

I looked at Douglas and shook my head.

"Ordinarily," I said, "I'd be truly pissed at you for going off like that and not telling them where you were going or when you'd be home. But since they were so worried about you, they forgot to be mad at me, I will forgive you, this time."

"Well," Douglas said. "That's gracious of you." We went up the porch steps together, and he looked down at the pompons in my hand. "Who do you think you are?" he wanted to know. "Marcia Brady?"

"No," I said with a sigh. "Madame Zenda."

CHAPTER

10

It didn't work, of course.

The pompons, I mean. All I got from them was a big fat nothing . . . and some of those streamery things up my nose, from when I tried sniffing them.

This isn't as weird as it sounds, since the vision I'd had about Shane seemed to have had an olfactory trigger. But what had worked with Shane's pillow most definitely did not work with Heather's pompons.

Maybe because I had actually liked Shane, and had felt responsible when he'd run away from the cabin we'd shared.

But Heather? Yeah, don't like her so much. And don't really feel responsible for her disappearing, either.

So why couldn't I fall asleep? I mean, if I felt so damned not responsible for what had happened to Heather, why was I lying there, staring at the ceiling?

Gee, I don't know. Maybe it was because of all the phone calls I'd gotten that evening, demanding to know why I hadn't found her already. Seriously, if I'd heard from every single member of the pep squad—with the exception of Heather and Amber, of course—I would not have been surprised. My mom, who was already in what could in no way be described as a good mood, on account of Mrs. Hankey's pending lawsuit against me and Douglas's sudden streak of wanderlust, threatened to disconnect the phone if it rang one more time.

Finally I was like, Go ahead, because I was sick of telling people I didn't know anything. It was bad enough the entire student population of Ernest Pyle High seemed to think I was still in full possession of my psychic powers. Now they apparently thought that I was refusing to use them for certain people, because I resented their popularity.

"Oh, no," Ruth said when I called her to tell her what was going on. "They did not say that to you."

"Yeah," I said. "They did. Tisha came right out with it. She was all, 'Jess, if you're holding back on us because of what Heather said to you in the caf the other day, may I just point out that she has been on the Homecoming court two years running, and that it would behoove you to get to work.'"

Ruth said, "Tisha Murray did not say the word *'behoove.'"*

"Well," I said. "You know what I mean."

"So I guess this means Mark didn't kill Amber after all." I heard a scratching sound, which meant that Ruth was filing her nails as she talked, as was her custom. "I mean, if he was with you when Heather disappeared."

"I guess," I said.

"Which means, you know. He's Do-able."

"He's not just Do-able," I said. "He's a hottie. And I think he kind of likes me." I told Ruth about how Mark had squeezed my hand and winked before leaving me to my fate with my parents. I did not mention that he seemed to have no goals other than making it to the pros. This would not have impressed Ruth.

"Wow," Ruth said. "If you start going out with the Cougars' quarterback, do you have any idea what kind of parties and stuff you're going to get invited to? Jess, you could run for Homecoming Queen. And maybe even win. If you grew your hair out."

"One thing at a time," I said. "First I have to prove he didn't kill his last girlfriend, by finding the guy who did. And," I added, "besides. What about Rob?"

"What *about* Rob?" Ruth demanded. "Jess, Rob's totally dissed you, all right? It's been three whole days since you got back, and he hasn't even called. Forget the Jerk. Go out with the quarterback. He's never been arrested for anything."

"Yet," I said.

"Jess, he didn't do it. This thing with Heather proves it."

There was a click, and then Skip went, "Hello? Hello? Who's using this line?"

"Skip," Ruth said, with barely suppressed fury. "I am on the phone."

"Oh, yeah?" Skip said. "With who?"

"With whom," Ruth thundered. "And I'm talking to Jess, all right? Now hang up. I'll be off in a minute."

"Hi, Jess," Skip said, instead of hanging up like he was supposed to.

"Hi, Skip," I said. "Thanks again for the ride this morning."

"Jess," Ruth roared. "DO NOT ENCOURAGE HIM!"

"I better go, I guess," Skip said. "Bye, Jess."

"Bye, Skip," I said. There was a click, and Skip was gone.

"You," Ruth said, "had better do something about this."

"Aw, Ruth," I said. "Don't worry about it. Skip and I are cool."

"No, you are not cool. He has a crush on you. I told you not to play so many video games with him, back at the lakehouse."

I wanted to ask her what else I'd been supposed to do, since she had never been around, but restrained myself.

"So what are you going to do now?" Ruth wanted to know.

"I don't know. Go to bed, I guess. I mean, by morning I'll know. Where Heather is, I mean."

"You hope," Ruth said. "You know, you've never looked for somebody you didn't like before. Maybe it only works with people you don't hold in complete contempt."

"God," I said before hanging up, "I hope that's not true."

But apparently it was, because when I did wake up, after seeming to have nodded off somewhere around midnight, I did not even remember I was supposed to be finding Heather. All I could think was, *Now what was that?*

This was because I'd wakened, not to the sound of my alarm, or the twittering of birds outside my bedroom window, but to a sharp, rattling noise.

Seriously. I opened my eyes, and instead of morning light pouring into my room, there was nothing but shadow. When I turned my head to look at my alarm clock, I saw why. It was only two in the morning.

Why, I wondered, had I woken up at two? I never wake up in the middle of the night for no reason. I am a sound sleeper. Mike always joked that a twister could rip through town, and I wouldn't so much as roll over.

Then I heard it again, what sounded like hailstones against my window.

Only they weren't hailstones, I realized this time. They were actual stones. Someone was throwing *rocks* at my window.

I threw back the blankets, wondering who on

earth it could be. Heather's friends were the only people I knew who might be anxious enough to see me to pull a stunt like this. But none of them had any way of knowing that my bedroom was the only one in the house that faced the street, or that it was the one with the dormer windows.

Staggering to one of those windows, I peered through the screen. Somebody, I saw, was standing in my front yard. There was hardly any moon, but from what little light it shed, I could see that the figure was tall and distinctly male—the distance across the shoulders was too wide for it to be a girl.

What guy did I know, I wondered, who would throw a bunch of rocks at my windows in the middle of the night? What guy did I know who even knew where my bedroom windows were?

Then it hit me.

"Skip," I hissed down at the figure in my yard. "What the hell do you think you're doing? Go home!"

The figure tipped his face up toward me and hissed back, "Who's Skip?"

I jumped back from the window with a start. That wasn't Skip. That wasn't Skip at all.

My heart slamming in my chest, I stood in the center of my bedroom, uncertain what to do. This had never happened to me before, of course. I was not the kind of girl who had guys tossing pebbles at her window every night. Claire Lippman, maybe, was used to that sort of thing, but I was not. I didn't know what to do.

"*Mastriani,*" I heard him call in a loud stage whisper.

There was no chance, of course, of him waking my parents, whose room was all the way at the opposite end of the house. But he might wake Douglas, whose windows looked out toward the Abramowitzes', and who was a light sleeper besides. I didn't want Douglas waking up and finding out that his little sister had a nocturnal caller. Who knew if that kind of thing might cause an episode.

I darted forward and, leaning over the sill, with my face pressed up against the screen, called softly, "Stay there. I'll be right down."

Then I spun around and reached for the first articles of clothing I could find—my jeans and a T-shirt. Slipping into some sneakers, I hopped down the hall to the bathroom, where I rinsed my mouth with some water and toothpaste— hey, a lady does not greet her midnight callers with morning breath. That much I *do* know about these things.

Then I crept down the stairs, carefully avoiding the notoriously creaky step just before the second landing, until I reached the front door and quietly unlocked it.

Then I stepped into the cool night air and Rob's warm embrace.

Look, I know, okay? Three days. *Three days* I'd been home, and he hadn't called. I should have been mad. I should have been livid. At the very least, I should have greeted him with cold civility, maybe a sneer and a "Hey, how you doing," instead of how I did greet him, which was by throwing my arms around him.

But I just couldn't help myself. He just looked so adorable standing there in the moonlight, all big and tall and manly and everything. You could tell he'd just taken a shower, because the dark hair on the back of his head was still wet, and he smelled of soap and shampoo and Goop, that stuff mechanics use on their hands to get the grease and motor oil out from beneath their nails. How could I not jump into his arms? You'd have done the exact same thing.

Except that Rob must have been supremely unaware of how stunningly hot he was, since he seemed kind of surprised to find me clinging to him the way those howler monkeys on the Discovery Channel cling to their mothers.

"Well," he said. He didn't exactly seem displeased. Just a little taken aback. "Hey. Nice to see you, too."

Well. Hey. Nice to see you, too. Not exactly what a girl expects to hear from the guy who has just woken her in the middle of the night by throwing pebbles at her bedroom window. A "Jess, I love you madly, run away with me" might have been nice. Heck, I'd have settled for an "I missed you."

But what did I get? Oh, no. That'd be a big "Well. Hey. Nice to see you, too."

I am telling you, my life *sucks.*

I let go of him and, since I was hanging about a foot in the air, Rob being that much taller than me, slithered back to the ground. Which I then stared at, in abject mortification. I had just, I could not help feeling, made a great big fool out of myself in front of him.

Again.

"Did I wake you up?" Rob wanted to know as we stood there on my front porch, awkward as two strangers, thanks to my underdeveloped social skills.

"Um," I muttered. "Yeah." What did he think? It was *two in the morning*. A perfect time, in my opinion, for a little romance.

But not, apparently, to Rob.

"Sorry," he said. He had shoved his hands into the pockets of his jeans, but not because he had to in order to keep himself from snatching me up and raining kisses down upon my face, like the heroes in the books I sometimes catch my mom reading, but rather because he didn't know what else to do with them. "I just found out you were back in town. My mom said you came into the restaurant tonight. Or last night, I guess."

Oh, God! His mother had told! Mrs. Wilkins had told him about waiting on me and Mark Leskowski at Table Seven. The make-out table! I sincerely hoped she'd mentioned that Mark and I had not, in point of fact, been making out.

"Yeah," I said. "I got back Sunday night. I had to. You know. School. It started on Monday."

What I did not add, though I wanted to, was, "You moron."

And I was glad I hadn't, when he said, "I

know. I mean, I figured it out tonight, that of course school must have started again. Last week of August and all. It's just that when you aren't going anymore, it's kind of hard to keep track."

Of course! Of course he hadn't known I was back! He wasn't in school anymore. How would he know it had started on Monday? And, being at work all day, it wasn't as if he'd have seen the buses, or anything.

So that's why he hadn't called or stopped by. Well, that and the fact that I'd asked him not to, on account of my parents not knowing about him, and all.

I gazed up at him, feelings of warmth and happiness coursing through me. Until Rob asked, "So, who's the guy?"

Oops.

The feelings of warmth and happiness vanished.

"Guy?" I echoed, stalling for time. A part of me was going, *Why, he's jealous! Ruth's stupid Rules thing actually works*, while another part went, *Hey, he's the one who insists on the two of you not dating, and now he's got a problem because you're seeing someone else? Tell him to deal with it*, while a third part of me felt sorry for hurting him, if indeed he was hurt, which was impossible to tell from his voice or expression, both of which were neutral.

Way neutral.

"Yeah," Rob said. "The one my mom saw you with."

"Oh, *that* guy," I said. "That's just, um, Mark."

"Mark?" Rob took his hand out of his pocket and ran his fingers through his still-damp hair. Which didn't, I decided, mean anything, really. "Yeah? You like him? This Mark guy?"

Oh, my God. I could not believe I was having this conversation. I mean, I was not the one with the problem with his arrest record and his age and all of that. *He* was the one who seemed to think he'd be robbing the cradle if he went out with me, even though he was only two years older and I am, I think, exceptionally mature for my age. And now he was upset because I'd gone out with somebody else—somebody else who, by the way, was his exact age, just minus the conviction?

So far, anyway.

I almost wished Ruth had been around to witness this. It was truly classic.

On the other hand, of course, I was wracked with guilt. Because if I'd had a choice between going out for pizza with Mark Leskowski and going to the dump to scrounge for used car parts with Rob Wilkins, I'd have chosen the dump any day of the week.

Which was why, a second later, I realized I could take it no longer. That's right, I broke the Rules. I ruined all that hard work, all that not calling, all that not chasing him, all that making him think I liked someone else, by saying, "Look, it's not what you think. Mark's girlfriend is the one who turned up dead on Sunday. I just went out with him to, you know, talk. The Feds are after him, now, see, so we have a lot in common."

Both of Rob's hands shot out of his pockets and landed, to my great surprise, on my shoulders. The next thing I knew, he was shaking me, rather hard.

"Mark Leskowski?" he wanted to know. "You went out with Mark Leskowski? Are you nuts? Are you trying to get yourself killed?"

"No," I said, between shakes. "He didn't do it."

"Bullshit!" Rob stopped shaking me. "Everyone knows he did it. Everyone except you, apparently."

I shushed him. "Do you want to wake my parents up?" I hissed. "That's the last thing I need, them finding me out on the front porch in the middle of the night with—"

"Hey," Rob said. "At least I'm not a murderer!"

"Neither is Mark," I said.

"Says you."

"No, says everyone. I know he didn't kill Amber, Rob, because while we were out together, another girl disappeared, Heather—"

I broke off with a gasp, as if somebody had pinched me. Pinched me? It felt more as if somebody had punched me.

"What is it?" Rob asked, grabbing my arm and looking down at me worriedly, all of his anger forgotten. "What's wrong, Jess? Are you all right?"

"I am," I said, when I had caught my breath. "But Heather Montrose isn't."

A fact I knew for certain, because the moment I'd uttered her name, I remembered the dream I'd been having, just as Rob's pebbles had woken me up.

Dream? What am I talking about? It had been a nightmare.

Except, of course, that it wasn't. A nightmare, I mean.

Because that was the thing. It had been real.

All too real.

CHAPTER

11

"Come on," I said to Rob as I darted down the porch steps into the yard. "We've got to get to her, before it's too late."

"Get to whom?" Rob followed me, looking confused. On him, of course, even confusion looked way sexy.

"Heather," I said, pausing by the dogwood tree at the end of the driveway. "Heather Montrose. She's the girl who disappeared this afternoon. I think I know where she is. We've got to go to her, now, before—"

"Before what?" Rob wanted to know.

I swallowed. "Before he comes back."

"Before who comes back? Jess, just what, exactly, did you see?"

I shivered, even though it couldn't have been much under seventy outside.

But it wasn't the temperature that was giving

me goosebumps. It was the memory of my dream about Heather.

Rob's question was a good one. Just what *had* I seen? Not much. Blackness, mostly.

It was what I had felt that had scared me most. And what I'd felt was surely what Heather was feeling.

Cold. That was one thing. Really, really cold.

And wet. And cramped. And in pain. A lot of pain, actually.

And fear. Fear that he was coming. Not just fear, either, but terror. Stark white terror, unlike anything I had ever known. That Heather had ever known, I mean.

No. That *we* had ever known.

"We've got to go," I said with a moan, my fingers sinking into his arm. Good thing I keep my nails short, or Rob would have been the one in some pain. "We've got to go *now.*"

"Okay," Rob said, prying my hand from his arm and taking it, instead, in his warm fingers. "Okay, whatever you say. You want to go find her? We'll go find her. Come on. My bike's over here."

Rob had parked his bike a little ways down the street. When we got to it, he opened up the compartment in the back and handed me his spare helmet and an extremely beat-up leather jacket he kept in there for emergencies, along with some other weird stuff, like a flashlight, tools, bottled water and, for reasons I'd never been able to fathom, a box of strawberry Nutri-

Grain bars. I think this was just because he liked them.

"Okay," he said, as I swung onto the seat behind him. "All set?"

I nodded, not trusting myself to speak. I was afraid if I did, I might start screaming. In my dream, that's what Heather had wanted to do. Scream.

Only she couldn't. Because there was something in her mouth.

"Uh, Mastriani?" Rob said.

I took a deep breath. All right. It was all right. It was happening to Heather, not to me.

"Yeah?" I asked, unsteadily. The sleeves of the leather jacket were way too long for me, and dangled past the hands I'd locked around his waist. I could feel Rob's heart beating through the back of his jean jacket. I tried to concentrate on that, rather than on the dripping sound that was the only thing Heather could hear.

"Where are we going?"

"Oh," I said. "P-Pike's Quarry."

Rob nodded, and a second later, the Indian roared to life, and we were off.

Ordinarily, of course, taking a moonlit motorcycle ride with Rob Wilkins would have been my idea of heaven on earth. I mean, let's face it: I am warm for the guy's form, and have been ever since that day in detention last year when he'd first asked me out, not knowing, of course, that I was only a sophomore and had never been out with a guy before in my life. By the time he'd figured it out, it was way too late. I was already smitten.

I like to think that the same could be said of him. And you know, the way he'd reacted when he'd heard I'd been out with another guy was kind of indicative that maybe he did like me as more than just a friend.

But I could no sooner rejoice over this realization than I could enjoy our ride. That, of course, was because of what I knew lay at the end of it. The road, I mean.

We did not encounter a single other vehicle along the way. Not until we reached the turnoff for the quarry, and saw a lone squad car sitting there with its interior light on as the officer within studied something attached to a clipboard. Rob slowed automatically as we approached—a speeding ticket he did not need—but didn't stop. His distrust of law enforcement agents is almost as finely honed as mine, only with better reason, since he'd actually been on the inside.

When we'd gotten far enough past the sheriff's deputy that we could pull over without him seeing us, Rob did say, keeping the motor running as he asked, "You want to ask him to join us?"

"Not yet," I said. "I'd rather . . . I want to make sure first."

Even though I was sure. Unfortunately, I was really sure.

"All right," Rob said. "Where to now?"

I pointed into the thick woods off to the side of

the road. The thick, dark, seemingly impenetrable woods to the side of the wood.

"Great," Rob said without enthusiasm. Then he put down his helmet's visor again and said, "Hang on."

It was slow going. The floor of the woods was soft with decaying leaves and pine needles, and the trees, only a few feet apart, made a challenging obstacle course. We could only see what was directly in front of the beam from the Indian's headlamp, and basically, all that was was trees, and more trees. I pulled back the sleeve of Rob's leather jacket and pointed whenever we needed to change directions.

Don't ask me, either, how I knew where we going, me—who can't read a map to save my life and who's managed to flunk my driving test twice. God knew I had never been in these woods before. I was not allowed, like Claire Lippman, to swim in the quarries, and had never been to them before. There was a reason swimming here was illegal, and that was because the dark, inviting water was filled with hidden hazards, like abandoned farm equipment with sharp spikes sticking up, and car batteries slowly leaking acid into the county's groundwater.

Sounds like paradise, huh? Well, to a bunch of teenagers who weren't allowed to drink beside their parents' pools, it was.

So even though I had never been here before, it was like . . . well, it was like I had. In my mind's eye, as Douglas would say, I had been here, and I knew where we going. I knew exactly.

Still, when we hit the road again, I was surprised. It wasn't even a road, exactly, just a strip of land that, decades before, had become flattened by the heavy limestone-removing equipment that had passed over it, day after day. Now it was really just a grass-strewn pair of ruts. Ruts that led up to a dirty, abandoned-looking house, all of the windowpanes of which were dark— and busted out—and which had a DANGER—KEEP OUT sign attached to the front door.

I signaled for Rob to stop, and he did. Then we both sat and stared at the house in the beam from his headlight.

"You have got," Rob said, switching off the engine, "to be kidding me."

"No," I said. I took off my helmet. "She's in there. Somewhere."

Rob pulled his own helmet from his head and sat for a minute, staring at the house. No sound came from it—or from anywhere, actually— except the chirping of crickets and the occasional hoo-hoo of an owl.

"Is she dead?" Rob asked. "Or alive?"

"Alive," I said. Then I swallowed. "I think."

"Is anybody in there with her?"

"I don't . . . I don't know."

Rob looked at the house for a minute more. Then he said, "Okay," and swung off the bike. He went to the back storage compartment and dug around in it. In the glow of the bike's head lamp and the dim light afforded from the tiny sliver of moon, I saw him pull out the flashlight, and something else.

A lug wrench.

He noticed the direction of my gaze.

"It never hurts," he said, "to be prepared."

I nodded, even though I doubted he could see this small gesture in the minimal moonlight.

"Okay," he said, closing the lid to the storage compartment and turning around to face me. "Here's how it's going to go down. I'm going to go in there and look around. If you don't hear from me in five minutes—oh, here, take my watch—you get on this bike and you go for that cop car we saw. Understand?"

I took his watch, but shook my head as I slipped it into the pocket of his leather jacket.

"No," I said. "I'm coming with you."

Rob's expression—what I could see of it, anyway—was eloquent with disapproval.

"Mastriani," he said. "Wait here. I'll be all right."

"I don't want to wait here." I couldn't, I knew very well, send him in to do what by rights should only have been done by me. I'd had the vision. I should be the one to go into the creepy house to see if the vision was real. "I want to come with you."

"Jess," Rob said. "Don't do this."

"I'm coming with you," I said. To my surprise, my voice broke. Really. Just like Tisha's had, when she'd gone into hysterics outside the Chocolate Moose. Was I, I wondered, going into hysterics?

If Rob heard the break in my voice, he gave no sign.

"Jess," he said, "you're staying here with the bike, and that's final."

"And what if," I asked, the break having turned into a throb, "they come back—if they aren't in there now—and find me out here all alone?"

I did not, of course, even remotely believe that this might happen, or that, in the unlikely event that it did, I would not be able to get away on the Indian, which went from zero to sixty in mere seconds, thanks to Rob's dedicated tinkering.

My question did, however, have the desired effect on Rob, in that he sighed and, hooking the lug wrench through one of the belt loops of his jeans, reached out and took my hand.

"Come on," he said, though he didn't look too happy about it.

The steps to the house's tiny front porch were nearly rotted through. We had to step carefully as we climbed them. I wondered who had lived here, if anyone. It might, I thought, have served as the management office during the time the limestone had been carved out of the quarry down the road. Certainly no one had lived in it for years. . . .

Though someone had certainly been inside recently, because the door, which had been nailed shut, swung easily under Rob's palm. In the bright beam from the Indian's headlamp, I could see the shiny points of the nails gleaming where they'd been pried from the wood, while their heads were nearly rusted through with weather and age.

Rob, shining his flashlight into the dank blackness past the door, muttered, "I have a really bad feeling about this."

I didn't blame him. I had a pretty creepy feeling about it myself. All I could hear were the crickets outside and the drumming of my own heart. And one other sound, much fainter than the other two. But, unfortunately, familiar. A dripping sound. Like water from a faucet that had not been properly shut off.

The drip, drip, drip from my dream.

I mean, my nightmare. Heather's reality.

Rob took a firmer grip on my hand, and we stepped inside.

We were not the first ones to have done so recently. Not by a long shot. In the first place, animals had clearly been making use of the space, leaving scattered droppings and nests of leaves and sticks all over the rotting wooden floor.

But raccoons and opossums weren't the dilapidated building's most recent tenants. Not if the many beer bottles and crumpled bags of chips on the floor were any indication. Someone had been doing some major partying. I could even smell, faintly, the intoxicating scent of human vomit.

"Nice," Rob said as we picked our way across the floor toward the only door, which hung crazily on its hinges. He paused and, letting go of my hand for a second, stooped to pick up a beer bottle.

"Imported," he said, reading the label by flashlight. Then he put the bottle down again. "Townies," he said, taking my hand again. "It figures."

The next room had apparently been a kitchen, but all of the fixtures were gone, except for a few rusted-out cabinets and a gas oven that looked beyond repair. There were less animal droppings in the kitchen, but more beer bottles, and, interestingly, a pair of pants. They were too big—and unstylish—to have belonged to Heather, so we continued our tour.

The kitchen led to the third and what I thought was the final room. This one had a fireplace, in which rested an empty keg.

"Someone," Rob said, "didn't care whether or not he got his deposit back."

That's when I noticed the stairs and tightened my grip on Rob's hand.

He followed the direction of my gaze, and sighed.

"Of course," he said. "Let's go."

The stairs were in only a little better condition than the porch steps. We climbed them slowly, taking care where we put each foot. One wrong step, and we'd have fallen through. As we climbed, the dripping sound grew steadily louder. Please, I prayed. Don't let that be blood.

The second floor consisted of three rooms. The first, to the left, had obviously been a bedroom at one time. There was still a mattress on the floor, though a mattress covered with so many stains and discolorations that I'd have only touched it with latex gloves on. A crunching noise beneath our feet revealed that my fears had not been ill-founded. There were condom wrappers everywhere.

"Well," Rob remarked, "at least they're practicing safe sex."

The second room was even worse. Here there was no mattress, just a couple of old blankets . . . but just as many condom wrappers.

I really thought I might be sick, and hoped the pizza Mark and I had consumed earlier had had time to digest.

Then there was just one last door, and I really, really didn't want Rob to open it, because I knew what we were going to find behind it. The dripping sound was coming from behind its closed door.

"Must be the bathroom," Rob said, and he let go of my hand to reach for the knob.

"No," I said, stepping forward. "No. Let me do it."

I couldn't see Rob's face in the darkness, but I could hear the concern in his voice as he said, "Sure . . . if you want to."

I gripped the doorknob. It felt cold beneath my palm.

Then the door flew open, and it was all exactly the way it had been in my vision. The dank, stained walls. The dark, windowless cell. The stained and ancient toilet, drip-drip-dripping.

And the figure curled up in the bathtub, her

mouth stretched into a hideous grin by the dirty strip of material holding the gag in place, her hair unkempt, her arms and legs twisted at painful angles by matching strips of material around her wrists and ankles.

It was only because of the purple and white uniform that I knew who she was at all. Well, that, of course, and my dream.

"Oh, Heather," I said, in a voice that didn't sound at all like my own. "I'm so sorry."

CHAPTER

12

"**J**esus," Rob said, holding the flashlight so that it shined on Heather's tear-stained face . . . which wasn't actually much help, since I was trying to loosen a knot at the back of her head, the one holding her gag in place, and I could barely see what I was doing.

"Rob," I said. I had crawled into the bathtub with Heather. "Hold the light over here, will you?"

He did as I asked, but it was like he was in a trance or something. I couldn't blame him, really. I mean, I'd had a pretty good feeling what kind of shape Heather would be in when we found her. He'd had no warning. No warning at all.

And it was bad. It was really bad. Worse even than I'd seen in my vision, because of course what I had seen, I had seen through Heather's eyes. I had not been able to see *her*, because in my dream, I'd *been* her.

Which was how I'd known she'd been in pain. Only now was I able to see why.

"Heather," I said when I'd gotten the gag out of her mouth. "Are you all right?"

It was a lame question, of course. She wasn't all right. The way she looked, I was willing to bet she'd never be all right again.

But what else was I supposed to say?

Heather didn't say anything. Her head lolled. She wasn't unconscious, but she was as close to it as a person could be.

"Here," Rob said, when he saw the trouble I was having with the knots at her wrists. He dug into his pocket and came up with a Swiss Army knife. It only took a second for the bright blade to sever the thin strip of material holding her hands behind her back.

It was only when one of those arms dangled limply after it was freed that I realized it was broken.

Not that Heather seemed to care, or notice, even. She'd balled up into a fetal position, and though Rob took his denim jacket off and draped it over her, she was shivering as if it were winter.

"I think she's in shock," Rob said.

"Yeah," I said. I'd heard things about shock. Like how shock alone could kill someone after an accident, even someone who was not all that seriously injured.

And Heather, if you asked me, was very seriously injured.

"Heather?" I peered into her face. It was hard

to tell whether or not she could hear me.
"Heather, can you hear me? Listen, it's all right.
Everything is going to be all right."

Rob gave it a try.

"Heather," he said. "You're safe now. Look,
can you tell us who did this? Can you tell us who
did this to you, Heather?"

That was when she finally opened her mouth.
But what came out was not the name of her
attacker.

"Go away," Heather wailed, pushing ineffec-
tually at me with her one unbroken arm. "Go
away before they come back . . . and find you
here. . . ."

Rob and I exchanged glances. In my concern
over Heather, I had forgotten that there was a
very strong possibility this could happen. You
know, that they might actually come back and
find us, I mean. I hoped Rob still had that wrench
handy.

"It's all right, Heather," I said, trying to calm
her. "Even if they do come back, they can't take
on all three of us."

"Yes, they can," Heather insisted. "Yes, they
can, yes, they can, yes, they can, yes . . ."

Okay, this was getting creepier by the minute.
I had thought, you know, we'd find her, and that
would be it.

But clearly, that was *not* it. There was a lot
more to it. Like, for instance, how the hell we
were going to get her out of there. No way was
she going to be able to stay on the bike in her

condition. I wasn't sure she could even sit up.

"Listen," I said to Rob. "You've got to go get that cop. The one by the turnoff? Tell him to call an ambulance."

Rob looked down at me like I was nuts. "Are you crazy?" he wanted to know. "You're the one who's going for the cop."

"Rob," I said, trying to keep my tone even and pleasant, so as not to alarm Heather, who seemed to have enough on her mind at the moment. "I am staying here with Heather. You are going for the cop."

"So you can get your arm broken like hers when they—whoever *they* are—come back?" Rob's tone was not even or pleasant. It was determined and grim-sounding. "Nuh-uh. I'm staying. You're going."

"Rob," I said. "No offense, but I think she'd be better off with someone she—"

But Rob didn't let me finish.

"And you'll be better off when you're miles away from here." Rob stood up and took me by the arm, half-lifting, half-dragging me out of the bathtub. "Come on."

I didn't want to go. Well, all right, I *did* want to go, but I didn't think I should go. I didn't want to leave Heather. I wasn't sure what, exactly, had happened to her, but whatever it had been, it had traumatized her to the point where I wasn't sure she even remembered her own name. How could I leave her alone with a guy she didn't know, especially since it was a fair guess that what had been done to her had been done by just that? Some random strange guy, I mean.

Or guys, I should say, since she'd said "they."

On the other hand, I didn't exactly want to stay with Heather alone while Rob went for help, either.

Fortunately, Rob made the decision for me. Bossy boyfriends do come in handy sometimes.

"You follow our tracks," he said when he'd pulled me down the stairs, through the party rooms, and out into the night air. "The tracks we made through the pine needles. See them? Follow those back to the road, then make a left. Got it? And do not stop. Do not stop for anything. When you find the guy, tell him to take the old pit road. Okay? The pit road. If he's local, he'll know what you're talking about."

He had shoved his helmet over my head, making speech difficult. Still, as I straddled the seat of the Indian, my feet barely reaching the boot rests, I tried to express my great unease with this plan.

Rob wasn't listening, however. He was busy starting the engine.

"Don't stop," he shouted again, when he'd successfully maneuvered the kickstart. "Do not stop for anyone not in uniform, understand?"

"But Rob," I said over the noise from the engine, which wasn't all that loud, actually, since Rob kept his bike in good repair. "I've never ridden on a motorcycle alone before. I'm not sure I know how."

"You'll be fine," he said.

"Um. I hesitate to mention this, but I think you should know, I don't exactly have a driver's license yet—"

"Don't worry about it. Just go."

He'd been holding on to the brake. Now he let go of it, and the bike jolted forward. My heart lurched as I grabbed for the handles. I was so short, I had to stretch out practically flat against the body of the bike to reach them . . . but reach them I did. I'd be all right, I realized . . . until I had to stop, anyway. No way were my short legs going to be able to reach the ground while still keeping the bike, which had to weigh eight hundred pounds, upright.

Rob had been right about one thing, anyway. I absolutely could not stop, and not because some of Heather's attackers might still be lurking around, but because once I stopped, I'd never be able to get the stupid thing up again.

And then I was careening back through the woods, trying to follow the ruts the Indian's wheels had made through the bracken on our way in from the road. It wasn't hard, exactly, to see where I was going—the headlight was bright enough that I could see a dozen or so feet ahead of me at all times. It was just that it was much harder to steer than I'd thought. My arms were straining with the effort of navigating the bike around all the trees that kept looming up in front of it.

This is what you always wanted, I told myself, as I drove. A bike of your own, to feel the wind on your face, to go as fast as you've always wanted, but no one would ever let you. . . .

Only when you are driving through the woods in the middle of the night looking for a cop, on your boyfriend's motorcycle that is, without a doubt, more bike than you can handle, you can't actually go very fast at all. Not if you don't want your wheels to spin out from beneath you.

My biggest fear was not that one of Heather's attackers might suddenly leap out at me from behind a tree, grab the handlebars of Rob's bike, and knock me to the ground. No, my biggest fear was that the engine was going to stall, because I was going so slowly.

I tried to kick up the speed a notch, and found that, by going another couple miles an hour faster, I could actually maneuver the bike much more easily. I tried not to concentrate so much on the trees, and instead concentrated on the open spaces around them. It sounds weird, but it actually helped. I figured it was like using the Force or something. *Trust your feelings, Jess,* I said to myself, in an Obi-Wan Kenobi voice. Know *the woods.* Feel *the woods.* Be *the woods.* . . .

I really hate the woods.

It was right after this that I burst out of the trees and skidded up the embankment to the road. There was a moment of panic when I thought I was going to tip over. . . .

But I threw out a foot and stopped myself at the last minute. I don't know how, but I managed to get the bike upright again and was off. The whole thing took barely a second, but in my mind, it seemed like an hour. My heart was thundering louder in my ears than the bike's engine.

Please be there, I was praying as I raced toward the place where we'd passed the squad car. *Please be there, please be there, please be there.* . . . Now that I was on the open road, I could really let loose, speedwise, and so I did, watching the speedometer go from ten, to twenty, to thirty, to forty. . . .

And then the squad car was looming up ahead of me, the overhead light still on, the cop inside, sipping a cup of coffee. The tinny sounds of the radio drifted out from the open window on the driver's side.

It was against the driver's side that I braced myself as I pulled up, to keep the bike from falling over.

"Officer," I said. I didn't have to say much to get his attention, because of course when someone on a motorcycle pulls up next to your car and leans on it, you notice right away.

"Yes?" The guy was young, probably only twenty-two or three. He still had acne. "What is it?"

"Heather Montrose," I said. "We found her back there, inside a house off that road, the old pit road, the one they don't use anymore. You better call an ambulance, she's really hurt."

The guy looked at me a minute, as if trying to figure out whether or not I was putting him on. I had Rob's helmet over my head, of course, so I don't know how much of my face he could make out. But what little he could see of me, he must have decided looked sincere, since he got on the radio and said he needed backup, along with an ambulance and paramedics. Then he looked at me and said, "Let's go."

It turned out the cops already knew about the house. They'd searched it, Deputy Mullins—that was his name—said, twice already, once right after Heather had been reported missing, and then again after nightfall. But they hadn't found anything suspicious inside . . . unless one counted a plethora of empty beer bottles and used condoms.

In any case, Deputy Mullins led me toward a clearly little-used dirt track just off the road. It was better, I found, than the way we'd originally taken through the woods, since I didn't have to dodge any trees. I wondered why my psychic radar hadn't led me this way before. Maybe because it ended up taking longer. It took us almost fifteen minutes of slow going over weedy, bumpy terrain to reach the house. It had only taken me ten minutes to get to the road through the woods. I knew from Rob's watch.

Deputy Mullins, when the house appeared in his headlights, pulled up beside it, then got on the radio again to describe his location. Then, leaving the headlights on, but his engine off, he got out of the car, while I leaned Rob's bike carefully against it, turned the engine off, and climbed down.

"She's in there," I said, pointing. "On the second floor."

Deputy Mullins nodded, but he looked nervous. Really nervous.

"Some people got her," I said. "She's afraid they might come back. She—"

Rob, having heard our approach, came out onto the porch. Deputy Mullins was even more nervous than I'd thought—either that, or the house was creeping him out as much as it had creeped me out—since he immediately went for his sidearm, sank down onto one knee, and, pointing the gun at Rob, yelled, "Freeze!"

Rob put both hands in the air and stood there, looking slightly bored, in the glare of the headlights.

May I just say that Rob Wilkins is the only person I know who would find having a gun drawn on him boring?

"Dude," I said to Deputy Mullins, in a voice high with suppressed emotion, "that's my boyfriend! He's—he's one of the good guys!"

Deputy Mullins lowered his gun. "Oh," he said, looking sheepish. "Sorry about that."

"It's cool," Rob said, putting his hands down. "Look, have you got a blanket and a first-aid kit in your car? She's not doing so hot."

Deputy Mullins nodded and raced around to the back of the squad car. I pulled my helmet off and hurried up to Rob.

"Did she say anything?" I asked him. "Like about who did it, or anything?"

"Not a word," Rob said. "All she'll talk about is how they—whoever they are—will be back soon, and how we're all going to be sorry when that happens."

"Yeah?" I said, running a hand through my sweaty hair. (It was hot inside that helmet.) "Well, I'm already sorry."

I was even more sorry when I led Deputy Mullins up the rickety stairs, and found out that, insofar as any sort of first aid knowledge was concerned, he was about as useless as Rob and me. All we could do was try to make her as warm and as comfortable as possible, then wait for the professionals.

It didn't take them long. It seemed as if no sooner had I crawled back into that bathtub than the wails from a half dozen sirens filled the night air. Seconds later, red lights were swirling across the inside walls of the house, like a lava lamp at a party, and voices could be heard outside. Deputy Mullins excused himself and went outside to show the EMT guys the way.

"Hear that, Heather?" I asked her, holding the hand on her unbroken arm. "That's the cops. Things are going to be okay now."

Heather only moaned. She obviously didn't believe me. It was almost as if she thought things were never going to be okay again.

Maybe she was right. At least, that's what I started to think as Rob and I, banished by the EMTs, who needed all the room to work on Heather that they could get in that cramped space, came down the stairs and onto the front porch. No, things weren't going to be okay. Not for a good long while, anyway.

Because Special Agents Johnson and Smith were coming toward us, their badges out and ready.

"Jessica," Special Agent Johnson said. "Mr. Wilkins. Will you two come with us, please?"

CHAPTER

13

"I told you," I said, for what had to have been the thirtieth time. "We were looking for a place to make out."

Special Agent Smith smiled at me. She was a very pretty lady, even when roused from her bed in the middle of the night. She had on pearl stud earrings, a crisply starched blue blouse, and black trousers. With her blonde bob and turned-up little nose, she looked perky enough to be a stewardess, or even a real-estate agent.

Except, of course, for the Glock 9 mm strapped to her side. That sort of detracted from the overall image of perkiness.

"Jess," she said, "Rob already told us that isn't true."

"Yeah," I said. "Well, of course he would say that, being a gentleman and all. But believe me, that's how it happened. We went in there to

154

make out, and we found Heather. And that's it."

"I see." Special Agent Smith looked down at the steaming cup of coffee she was holding between her hands. They'd offered me a cup, too, but I had declined. I didn't need my growth stunted anymore than it already had been thanks to my DNA.

"And do you and Rob," she went on, "always drive fifteen miles out of town just to make out?"

"Oh, yeah," I said. "It's more exciting that way."

"I see," Special Agent Smith said, again. "And the fact that Rob has the keys to his uncle's garage, where he works, and the two of you could have gone there, a place that is significantly closer and quite a bit cleaner than that house on the pit road . . . you still expect me to believe you?"

"Yes," I said, with some indignation. "We can't go to his uncle's garage to make out. Somebody might find out, and then Rob'd get fired."

Special Agent Smith propped her elbow up onto the table where we sat in the police station, then dropped her forehead into her hand.

"Jessica," she said, sounding tired. "You declined an invitation to your own best friend's lakehouse because you heard it didn't have cable television. Do you honestly expect me to believe that you would so much as enter a house like the one on the pit road if you didn't absolutely have to?"

I narrowed my eyes at her. "Hey," I said. "How'd you know about the cable thing?"

"We are the Federal Bureau of Investigation, Jess. We know everything."

This was distressing. I wondered if they knew about Mrs. Hankey's lawsuit. I figured they probably did.

"Well," I said. "Okay. I admit it's a little gross in there. But—"

"A little gross?" Special Agent Smith sat up straight. "I'm sorry, Jessica, but I think I'm well enough acquainted with you to know that if any boy—but especially, I suspect, Rob Wilkins—took you into a house like that to be intimate, we'd have a homicide on our hands. Namely, his."

I tried to take umbrage at this assessment of my personality, but the fact was, Jill was right. I could not understand how any girl would let a boy take her to such a place. Better to get down and dirty in his *car* than in that disgusting frat house.

Frat house? *Rat* house was more like it.

I am certainly not saying that if a girl is going to lose her virginity, it has to be on satin sheets or something. I am not *that* big of a prude. But there should at least *be* sheets. Clean ones. And no refuse from trysts past lying around on the floor. And a person should at least take his empty beer bottles to the recycling plant before even thinking of entertaining. . . .

Oh, what was the point? She had me, and she knew it.

"So can we please," Special Agent Smith said,

"drop this ridiculous story that you and Mr. Wilkins went to that house in order to get hot and heavy? We know better, Jessica. Why won't you just admit it? You knew Heather was in that house, and that's why you and Rob went there."

"I swear—"

"Admit it, Jessica," Jill said. "You had a vision you'd find her there, didn't you?"

"I did not," I said. "You can ask Rob. We went to—"

"We did ask Rob," Special Agent Smith said. "He said that the two of you went to the quarry to look for Heather and just happened to stumble across the house."

"And that's exactly how it did happen," I said, proud that Rob had thought up such a good story. It was far better, I realized, than my make out story. Though I certainly *wished* my make-out story was true.

"Jessica, I sincerely hope, for your sake, that that isn't true. The whole idea of you two just stumbling over a kidnapping victim *accidentally* strikes us as . . . well, as a little suspicious, to say the least."

I narrowed my eyes at her. I still had Rob's watch with me—it wasn't like we were under arrest or anything, and they'd taken all of our valuables to hold for safekeeping. Oh, no. We were just being held for *questioning.*

Which was what Special Agents Johnson and Smith had been doing for the past two hours. *Questioning* us.

And now it was close to dawn, and you know what? I was really, really tired of being *questioned.*

But not so tired that I missed the implication in her words.

"What do you mean, it sounds 'suspicious'?" I demanded. "What are you suggesting?"

Special Agent Smith only regarded me thoughtfully with her pretty blue eyes.

I let out a laugh, even though I didn't really see anything all that funny about it.

"Oh, I get it," I said. "You think Rob and I did it? You think Rob and I kidnapped Heather and beat her up and left her for dead in that bathtub? Is that what you think?"

"No," Special Agent Smith said. "Mr. Wilkins was working in his uncle's garage at the time Heather first disappeared. We have a half dozen witnesses who will attest to that. And you, of course, were with Mr. Leskowski. Again, we have quite a number of people who saw you two together."

My jaw sagged. "Oh, my God," I said. "You checked on my alibi? You didn't wake Mrs. Wilkins up, did you? Tell me you didn't call Rob's mom and wake her up. Jill, how could you? Talk about embarrassing!"

"Frankly, Jessica," Special Agent Smith said, "your embarrassment doesn't concern me at all. All I am interested in is finding out the truth. How did you know Heather Montrose was in that house? The police searched there twice after learning another girl had disappeared. They didn't find anything. So how did you know to look there?"

I glared at her. Really, it was one thing to have the Feds following you around and reading your mail and tapping your phone and all. It was quite another to have them going around, waking up your future mother-in-law in the middle of the night to ask questions about your dinner with another boy, who wasn't even her son.

"Okay, that's it," I said, folding my arms across my chest. "I want a lawyer."

It was at this point that the door to the little interrogation room—a conference room, Special Agent Smith had called it, but I knew better—opened, and her partner came in.

"Hello, again, Jessica," he said, dropping into a chair beside me. "What do you want a lawyer for? You haven't done anything wrong, have you?"

"I'm a minor," I said. "You guys are required to question me in the presence of a parent or guardian."

Special Agent Johnson sighed and dropped a file onto the tabletop. "We've already called your parents. They're waiting for you downstairs."

I nearly beat my head against something. I couldn't believe it. "You told my *parents?*"

"As you pointed out," Special Agent Johnson said, "we are required to question you in the presence—"

"I was just giving you a hard time," I cried. "I can't believe you actually called them. Do you have any idea how much trouble I'm going to be in? I mean, I completely snuck out of the house in the middle of the night."

"Right," Special Agent Johnson said. "Let's talk about that for a minute, shall we? Just why *did* you sneak out? It wasn't, by any chance, because you'd had another one of your psychic visions, was it?"

I couldn't believe this. I really couldn't. Here Rob and I had done this fabulous thing—we'd saved this girl's life, according to the EMTs, who said that Heather, though she was only suffering from a broken arm and rib and some severe bruising, would have been dead by morning due to shock if we hadn't come along and found her—and all anybody could do was harp on how we'd known where she was. It wasn't fair. They should have been throwing a *parade* for us, not interrogating us like a couple of miscreants.

"I told you," I said. "I don't have ESP anymore, okay?"

"Really?" Special Agent Johnson flipped open the file he'd put on the table. "So it wasn't you who put in the call to 1-800-WHERE-R-YOU yesterday morning, telling them where they could find Courtney Hwang?"

"Never heard of her," I said.

"Right. They found her in San Francisco. It appears she was kidnapped from her home in Brooklyn four years ago. Her parents had just about given up hope of ever seeing her again."

"Can I go home now?" I demanded.

"A call was placed to 1-800-WHERE-R-YOU at approximately eight in the morning yesterday from the Dunkin' Donuts down the street from the garage where Mr. Wilkins works. But you wouldn't know anything about that, of course."

"I lost my psychic abilities," I said. "Remember? It was on the news."

"Yes, Jessica," Special Agent Johnson said. "We are aware that you told reporters that. We are also aware that, at the time, your brother Douglas was experiencing some, shall we say, troublesome symptoms of his schizophrenia, that were perhaps exacerbated by the stress of your being so persistently pursued by the press. . . ."

"Not just the press," I said, with some heat. "You guys had a little something to do with it, too, remember?"

"Regrettably," Special Agent Johnson said, "I do. Jessica, let me ask you something. Do you know what a profile is?"

"Of course I do," I said. "It's when law enforcement officers go around arresting people who fit a certain stereotype."

"Well," Special Agent Johnson said, "yes, but that's not exactly what I meant. I meant a formal summary or analysis of data, representing distinctive characteristics or features."

"Isn't that what I just said?" I asked.

"No."

Special Agent Johnson didn't have much of a sense of humor. His partner was much more fun . . . though that wasn't saying much. Allan Johnson, it had often occurred to me, just might be the most boring person on the entire planet. Everything about him was boring. His mouse-colored hair, thinning slightly on top and parted on the right, was boring. His glasses, plain old steel frames, were boring. His suits, invariably charcoal gray, were boring. Even his ties, usually in pale blues or yellows, without a pattern, were boring. He was married, too, which was the most boring thing about him of all.

"A profile," Special Agent Johnson said, "of the type of person who might commit a crime like the ones we've experienced this week—the strangulation of Amber Mackey, for instance, and the kidnapping of Heather Montrose—might sound something like this: He is most likely a white heterosexual male, in his late teens or early twenties. He is intelligent, perhaps highly so, and yet suffers from an inability to feel empathy for his victims, or anyone, for that matter, save himself. While he might seem, to his friends and family, to be a normal, even high-functioning member of society, he is, in fact, wracked with inner misgivings, perhaps even paranoia. In some cases, we have found that killers like this one act the way they do because inner voices, or visions, direct them to—"

That's when it hit me. I'd be listening to his little speech, going, Hmmm, white heterosexual male, late teens, sounds like Mark Leskowski, highly intelligent, inability to feel empathy, yeah, that could be him. He's a football player, after all, but a quarterback, which takes some smarts, anyway. Then there's that whole "unacceptable" thing.

Only it can't be him, because he was with me when Heather was kidnapped. And according to the EMTs, those wounds she'd sustained were a good six hours old, which meant whoever had done it—and Heather still wasn't talking—had attacked her at around eight in the evening. And Mark had been with me at eight. . . .

But when Allan got to the part about inner voices, I sat up a little straighter.

"Hey," I said. "Wait just a minute here. . . ."

"Yes?" Special Agent Johnson broke off and looked at me expectantly. "Something bothering you, Jessica?"

"You've got to be kidding me," I said. "You can't seriously be trying to pin this thing on my brother."

Jill looked thoughtful. "Why on earth would you think we were trying to do that, Jess?"

My jaw dropped. "What do you think I am, stupid or something? He just said—"

"I don't see what would make you jump to the conclusion," Special Agent Johnson said, "that we suspect Douglas, Jessica. Unless you know something we don't know."

"Yes," Special Agent Smith said. "Did Douglas tell you where you could find Heather, Jessica? Is that how you knew to look in the house on the pit road?"

"Oh!" I stood up so fast, my chair tipped over backwards. "That's it. That is so it. End of interview. I am out of here."

"Why are you so angry, Jessica?" Special

Agent Johnson, not moving from his chair, asked me. "Could it be perhaps because you think we might be right?"

"In your dreams," I said. "You are *not* pinning this one on Douglas. *No way.* Ask Heather. Go ahead. She'll tell you it wasn't Douglas."

"Heather Montrose did not see her attackers," Special Agent Johnson said lightly. "Something heavy was thrown over her head, she says, and then she was locked in a small enclosed space— presumably a car trunk—until some time after nightfall. When she was released, it was by several individuals in ski masks, from whom she attempted to escape—but who dissuaded her most emphatically. She can only say that their voices sounded vaguely familiar. She recalls very little, other than that."

I swallowed. Poor Heather.

Still, as a sister, I had a job to do.

"It wasn't Douglas," I said vehemently. "He doesn't have any friends. And he certainly has never owned a ski mask."

"Well, it shouldn't be hard to prove he had nothing to do with it," Special Agent Smith said. "I suppose he was in his room the whole time, as usual. Right, Jessica?"

I stared at them. They knew. I don't know how, but they knew. They knew Douglas hadn't been in the house when Heather had disappeared.

And they also knew I hadn't the slightest idea where he'd been, either.

"If you guys," I said, feeling so mad it was a

wonder smoke wasn't coming out of my nostrils, "even *think* about dragging Douglas into this, you can kiss good-bye any hope you might have of me ever coming to work for you."

"What are you saying, Jessica?" Special Agent Johnson asked. "That you do, indeed, still have extrasensory perception?"

"How did you know where to find Heather Montrose, Jessica?" Jill asked in a sharp voice.

I went to the door. When I got to it, I turned around to face them.

"You stay away from Douglas," I said. "I mean it. If you go near him—if you so much as *look* at him—I'll move to Cuba, and I'll tell Fidel Castro everything he ever wanted to know about your undercover operatives over there."

Then I flung the door open and stalked out into the hallway.

Well, they couldn't stop me. I wasn't under arrest, after all.

I couldn't believe it. I really couldn't. I mean, I knew the United States government was eager to have me on its payroll, but to stoop to suggesting that if I did not come to their aid, they would frame my own brother for a crime he most certainly did not commit . . . well, that was low. George Washington, I knew, would have hung his head in shame if he'd heard about it.

When I got to the waiting area, I was still so mad I almost went stalking right through it, right out the door and on down the street. I couldn't see properly, I was so mad.

Or maybe it was because I'd just gone for so long without sleep. Whatever the reason, I stalked right past Rob and my parents, who were waiting for me—on different sides of the room—in front of the duty desk.

"Jessica!"

My mother's cry roused me from my fury. Well, that and the fact that she flung her arms around me.

"Jess, are you all right?"

Caught up in the stranglehold that served as my mother's excuse for a hug, I blinked a few times and observed Rob getting up slowly from the bench he'd been stretched out across.

"What happened?" my mom wanted to know. "Why did they keep you in there for so long? They said something about you finding a girl— another cheerleader. What's this all about? And what on earth were you doing out so late?"

Rob, across the room, smiled at the eye-roll I gave him behind my mother's back. Then he mouthed, "Call me."

Then he—very tactfully, I thought—left.

But not tactfully enough, since my dad went, "Who was that boy over there? The one who just left?"

"No one, Dad," I said. "Just a guy. Let's go home, okay? I'm really tired."

"What do you mean, just a guy? That wasn't even the same boy you were with earlier. How many boys are you seeing, anyway, Jessica? And what, exactly, were you doing out with him in the middle of the night?"

"Dad," I said, taking him by the arm and trying to physically propel him and my mother from the station house. "I'll explain when we get to the car. Now just come on."

"What about the rule?" my father demanded.

"What rule?"

"The rule that states you are not to see any boy socially whom your mother and I have not met."

"That's not a rule," I said. "At least, nobody ever told me about it before."

"Well, that's just because this is the first time anyone's asked you out," my dad said. "But you can bet there are going to be some rules now. Especially if these guys think it's all right for you to sneak out at night to meet with them—"

"Joe," my mother whispered, looking around the empty waiting room nervously. "Not so loud."

"I'll talk as loud as I want," my dad said. "I'm a taxpayer, aren't I? I paid for this building. Now I want to know, Toni. I want to know who this boy is our daughter is sneaking out of the house to meet. . . ."

"God," I said. "It's Rob Wilkins." I was more glad than I could say that Rob wasn't around to hear this. "Mrs. Wilkins's son. Okay? Now can we go?"

"Mrs. Wilkins?" My dad looked perplexed. "You mean Mary, the new waitress at Mastriani's?"

"Yes," I said. "Now let's—"

"But he's much too old for you," my mother

said. "He's graduated already. Hasn't he graduated already, Joe?"

"I think so," my dad said. You could tell he was totally uninterested in the subject now that he knew he employed Rob's mother. "Works over at the import garage, right, on Pike's Creek Road?"

"A garage?" my mother practically shrieked. "Oh, my God—"

It was, I knew, going to be a long drive home.

"This," my father said, "had better have been one of those ESP things, young lady, or you—"

And an even longer day.

CHAPTER

14

I didn't get to school until fourth period.

That's because my parents, after I'd explained about rescuing Heather, let me sleep in. Not that they were happy about it. Good God, no. They were still excessively displeased, particularly my mother, who did NOT want me hanging out anymore with a guy who had no intention, now or ever, of going to college.

My dad, though . . . he was cool. He was just like, "Forget it, Toni. He's a nice kid."

My mom was all, "How would you know? You've never even met him."

"Yeah, but I know Mary," he said. "Now go get some sleep, Jessica."

Except that I couldn't. Sleep, that is. In spite of the fact that I lay in my bed from five, when I finally crawled back into it, until about ten thirty. All I could think about was Heather and that

169

house. That awful, awful house.

Oh, and what Special Agent Johnson had said, too. About Douglas, I mean.

All Douglas's voices ever do is tell him to kill himself, not other people.

So it didn't make sense, what Special Agent Johnson was suggesting. Not for a minute.

Besides, Douglas didn't even drive. I mean, he had a license and a car and all.

But since that day they'd called us—last Christmas, when Douglas had had the first of his episodes, up where he was going to college— and we went to get him, and Mike drove his car back, it had sat, cold and dead, under the carport. Even Mike—who'd have given just about anything for a car of his own, having stupidly asked for a computer for graduation instead of a car, with which he might have enticed Claire Lippman, his lady love, on a date to the quarries—wouldn't touch Douglas's car. It was Douglas's car. And Douglas would drive it again one day.

Only he hadn't. I knew he hadn't because when I went outside, after Mom offered to give me a lift to school, I checked his tires. If he'd been driving around out by that pit house, there'd have been gravel in them.

But there wasn't. Douglas's wheels were clean as a whistle.

Not that I'd believed Special Agent Johnson. He'd just been saying that about Douglas to see if I maybe knew who the real killer was and just wasn't telling, for some bizarre reason. As if anybody who knew the identity of a murderer would go around keeping it a secret.

I am so sure.

I got to Orchestra in the middle of the strings' chair auditions. Ruth was playing as I walked in with my late pass in hand. She didn't notice me, she was so absorbed in what she was playing, which was a sonata we'd learned at music camp that summer. She would, I knew, get first chair. Ruth always gets first chair.

When she was done, Mr. Vine said, "Excellent, Ruth," and called the next cellist. There were only three cellists in Symphonic Orchestra, so it wasn't like the competition was particularly rough. But we all had to sit there and listen while people auditioned for their chairs, and let me tell you, it was way boring. Especially when we got to the violins. There were about fifteen violinists, and they all played the same thing.

"Hey," I whispered, as I pretended to be rooting around in my backpack for something.

"Hey," Ruth whispered back. She was putting her cello away. "Where were you? What's going on? Everyone is saying you saved Heather Montrose from certain death."

"Yeah," I said modestly. "I did."

"Jeez," Ruth said. "Why am I always the last to know everything? So where was she?"

"In this disgusting old house," I whispered back, "on the pit road. You know, that old road no one ever uses anymore, off Pike's Quarry."

"What was she doing there?" Ruth wanted to know.

"She wasn't exactly there by choice." I explained how Rob and I had found Heather.

"Jeez," Ruth said again, when I was through. "Is she going to be all right?"

"I don't know," I said. "Nobody will say. But—"

"Excuse me. Would you two please keep it down? You are ruining this for the rest of us."

We both looked over and saw Karen Sue Hankey shooting us an annoyed look.

Only she was shooting it at us over a wide, white gauze bandage, which stretched across her nose and was stuck in place on either cheekbone with surgical tape.

I burst out laughing. Well, you would have, too.

"Laugh all you want, Jess," Karen Sue said. "We'll see who's laughing last in court."

"Karen Sue," I choked, between chortles. "*What* have you got that thing on for? You look completely ridiculous."

"I am suffering," Karen Sue said, primly, "from a contused proboscis. You can see the medical report."

"Contused pro—" Ruth, who'd gotten a perfect score on the verbal section of her PSATs, went, "For God's sake. All that means is that your nose is bruised."

"The chance of infection," Karen Sue said, "is dangerously high."

That one killed me. I nearly convulsed, I was

laughing so hard. Mr. Vine finally noticed and said, "*Girls,*" in a warning voice.

Karen Sue's eyes glittered dangerously over the edge of her bandage, but she didn't say anything more.

Then.

When the bell for lunch finally rang, Ruth and I booked out of there as fast as we could. Not, of course, because we were so eager to sample the lunch fare being offered in the caf, but because we wanted to talk about Heather.

"So she said '*they,*'" Ruth said as we bent over our tacos, the entree of the day. Well, I bent over my taco. Ruth had crumbled hers all up with a bunch of lettuce and poured fat-free dressing all over it, making a taco salad. And a mess, in my opinion. "You're sure about that? She said, '*They're* coming back'?"

I nodded. I was starving, for some reason. I was on my third taco.

"Definitely," I said, swilling down some Coke. "*They.*"

"Which makes it seem likely," Ruth said, "that more than one person was involved in Amber's attack, as well. I mean, if the two attacks are related. Which, face it, they must be."

"Right," I said. "What I want to know is, who's been using that house as their party headquarters? Somebody's been letting loose there, and pretty regularly, from the looks of it."

Ruth shuddered delicately. I had, of course, described the house on the pit road in all its lurid detail . . . including the condom wrappers.

"While I suppose we should be grateful, at least, that they—whoever *they* are—are practicing safe sex," Ruth said with a sigh, "it hardly seems like the kind of place one might refer to as a love shack."

"No kidding," I said. "The question is who have they—whoever *they* are—been taking there? Girl-wise, I mean. Unless, you know, they're having sex with each other."

Ruth shook her head. "Gay guys would have fixed the place up. You know, throw pillows and all of that. And they would have recycled their empties."

"True," I said. "So what kind of girl would put up with those kind of conditions?"

We looked around the caf. Ernest Pyle High was, I suppose, a pretty typical example of a midwestern American high school. There was one Hispanic student, a couple of Asian-Americans, and no African-Americans at all. Everyone else was white. The only difference between the white students, besides religion—Ruth and Skip, being Jewish, were in the minority—was how much their parents earned.

And that, as usual, turned out to be the crux of the matter.

"Grits," Ruth said simply, as her gaze fell upon a long table of girls whose perms were clearly of the at-home variety, and whose nails were press-on, not salon silk-wrapped. "It has to be."

"No," I said.

Ruth shook her head. "Jess, why not? It makes sense. I mean, the house is way out in the country, after all."

"Yeah," I said. "But the beer bottles on the floor. They were imports."

"So?"

"So Rob and his friends"—I swallowed a mouthful of taco—"they only drink American beer. At least, that's what he said. He saw the bottles and went, 'Townies.'"

Ruth eyed me. "Has it ever occurred to you that the Jerk might be covering up for his bohunk friends?"

"Rob," I said, putting my taco down, "is not a jerk. And his friends aren't bohunks. If you will recall, they saved me from becoming the U.S. Army's number one secret weapon last spring. . . ."

"I am not trying to be offensive," Ruth said. "Honest, Jess. But I think you might be too besotted with this guy to see the writing on the wall—"

"The only writing I'm looking at," I said, "is the writing that says Rob didn't do it."

"I am not suggesting that he did. I am merely saying that some of his peers might—"

Suddenly an enormous backpack plonked down onto the bench beside mine. I looked up and had to restrain a groan.

"Hi, girls," Skip said. "Mind if I join you?"

"Actually," Ruth said, her upper lip curling. "We were just leaving."

"Ruth," Skip said, "You're lying. I have never seen you leave a taco salad unfinished."

"There's a first time for everything," Ruth said.

"Actually," Skip said, "what I have to say will only take a minute. I know how you girls value your precious dining moments together. There's a midnight screening of a Japanese anime film at the Downtown Cinema this weekend, and I wanted to know if you'd be interested in going."

Ruth looked at her brother as if he'd lost his mind. "*Me?*" she said. "You want to know if *I*'d go to the movies with you?"

"Well," Skip said, looking, for the first time since I'd known him—and that was a long, long time—embarrassed. "Not you, actually. I meant Jess."

I choked on a piece of taco shell.

"Hey," Skip said, banging me on the back a few times. "You all right?"

"Yeah," I said, when I'd recovered. "Um. Listen. Can get I back to you on that? The movie thing, I mean? I've kind of got a lot going on right now. . . ."

"Sure," Skip said. "You know the number." He picked up his backpack and left.

"Oh . . . my . . . God," Ruth said as soon as he was out of earshot. I told her to shut up.

Only she didn't.

"He loves you," Ruth said. "Skip is in love with you. I can't believe it."

"Shut up, Ruth," I said, getting up and lifting my tray.

"Jessica and Skip, sittin' in a tree." Ruth could not stop laughing.

I walked over to the conveyor belt that carries

our lunch trays into the kitchen and dumped it. As I was dumping it, I saw Tisha Murray and a few of the other cheerleaders and jocks—and Karen Sue, who followed the popular crowd wherever they went, thus making her deserving of Mark's nickname for her, the Wannabe—leaving the caf. They were going outside to lounge by the flagpole, which was where all the beautiful people in our school sat on nice days, working on their tans until the bell rang.

"Skip's never been out on a date before," Ruth said, coming up behind me to dump her own tray. "I wonder if he'll know not to bring his backpack along."

Ignoring Ruth, I followed Tisha and the others outside.

It was another gorgeous day—the kind that made sitting inside a classroom really hard. Summer was over, but somebody had forgotten to tell the weatherman. The sun beat down on the long, outstretched legs of the cheerleaders in the grass beneath the flagpole, and on the backs of the jocks who stood above them. I could not see Mark anywhere, but Tisha was sitting on the grass with one hand shading her eyes, talking to Jeff Day.

"Tisha," I said, going up to her.

She swung her face toward me, then gaped.

"Ohmigod," Tisha cried, scrambling to her feet. "There she is! The girl who saved Heather! Ohmigod! You are, like, a total and complete hero. You know that, don't you?"

I stood there awkwardly as everyone congratulated me for being such a hero. I don't think I'd ever been spoken to by so many popular kids all at once in my life. It was like, suddenly, I was one of them.

And gee, all I'd had to do was have a psychic vision about one of their friends, and then gone and saved her life.

See? Anyone can be popular. It's not hard at all.

"Tisha," I said, trying to be heard over the cacophony of excited voices around me. "Can I talk to you a minute?"

Tisha broke free from the others and came up to me, her tiny bird-head tilted questioningly. "Uh-huh, Ms. Hero," she said. "What is it?"

"Look, Tisha." I took her by the arm and started steering her, slowly, away from the crowd and toward the parking lot. "About that house. Where I found Heather. Did you know about that place?"

Tisha pushed some of her hair out of her eyes. "The house on the pit road? Sure. Everyone knows about that house."

I was about to ask her if she knew who'd scattered their beer bottles throughout the house, and what was up with that skanky old mattress, when I was distracted by a familiar sound. It was a sound that, for a long time now, my ears had become totally attuned to, separating it out from all other sounds.

Because it was the sound of Rob's engine.

Well, his motorcycle's engine, to be exact.

I turned around, and there he was, coming

around the corner and into the student lot, looking, I have to say, even better in daylight than he had the night before in moonlight. When he pulled up beside me, cut the engine, and took off his helmet, I thought my heart would burst at how handsome he looked in his jeans, motorcycle boots, and T-shirt, with his longish dark hair and bright gray eyes.

"Hey," he said. "Just the person I wanted to see. How are you doing?"

Conscious that the curious gazes of the entire student population of Ernest Pyle High School—well, at least the people who were enjoying the last minutes of their lunch break out of doors, anyway—were upon us, I said, casually, "Hi. I'm fine. How about you?"

Rob got off his bike and ran a hand through his hair.

"I'm okay, I guess," he said. "You're the one who got the third degree, not me. First from the Feds and then from your parents. Or am I wrong about that?"

"Oh, no," I said. "You're right. They weren't too happy. None of them. Allan and Jill *and* Joe and Toni."

"That's what I thought," Rob said. "So I figured I'd come over on my lunch break and, you know, see if you were all right. But you seem fine." His gray-eyed gaze skittered over me. "More than fine, actually. You dressed up for any particular reason?"

I had on another one of my new outfits from the

outlet stores. It consisted of a black V-neck cropped shirt, a pink miniskirt, and black platform sandals. I looked *très chic*, as they'd say in French class.

"Oh," I said, glancing down at myself. "Just, you know. Making an effort this year. Trying to stay out of trouble."

Rob, to my delight, scowled at the skirt. "I don't see that happening real soon, Mastriani," he said. Then his gaze strayed toward my wrist. "Hey. Is that my watch?"

Busted. So busted. I'd found his watch, a heavy black one, covered with buttons that did weird things like tell the time in Nicaragua and stuff, in the pocket of his leather jacket—a jacket that was now hanging in a place of honor off one of my bedposts.

Of course I'd worn it to school. What girl wouldn't?

"Oh, yeah," I said, with elaborate nonchalance. "You loaned it to me last night. Remember?"

"Now I do," Rob said. "I was looking everywhere for that. Hand it over."

Bumming excessively, I unstrapped it. I know it was ridiculous, me wanting to hang onto the guy's watch, of all things, but I couldn't help it. It was like my trophy. My boyfriend trophy.

Except, of course, that Rob wasn't really my boyfriend.

"Here you go," I said, handing it to him. He took it and put in on, looking down at me like I was demented or something. Which I probably am.

"Do you like this watch or something?" he wanted to know. "Do you want one like it?"

"No," I said. "Not really." I couldn't tell him the truth, of course. How could I?

"Because I could get you one," he said. "If you want. But I would think you'd want, you know, one of those ladies' watches. This one looks kind of stupid on you."

"I don't want a watch," I said. Just your watch.

"Well," he said. "Okay. If you're sure."

"I'm sure."

He looked down at me. "You're kind of weird," he said. "You know that, don't you?"

Oh, well, this was just great. My boyfriend rides all the way over on his lunch break to tell me he thinks I'm weird. How romantic.

Thank God Tisha and the rest of those guys were too far away to hear what he was saying.

"Well, look, I have to get back," he said. "You stay out of trouble. Leave the police work to the professionals, understand? And call me, okay?"

"Sure," I said.

He squinted at me in the sunlight. "Are you sure you're okay?"

"Yeah," I said.

But of course I wasn't. Well, I mean, I was, and I wasn't. What I really wanted was for him to kiss me. I know. Retarded, right? I mean, me wanting him to kiss me, just because Tisha and a whole bunch of people were watching.

But it was kind of like the reason I'd wanted to

hang onto his watch. I just wanted everyone to know I belonged to somebody.

And that that somebody was not Skip Abramowitz.

Now, I am not saying that Rob read my mind or anything. I mean, I'm the psychic, not him.

And I am not even saying that maybe I somehow put the suggestion in his head, either. My psychic powers extend toward one thing, and one thing only, and that's finding missing people, not putting suggestions into boys' heads that they should kiss me.

But be that as it may, Rob rolled his eyes, said, "Aw, screw it," wrapped a hand around the back of my neck, pulled me forward, and kissed me roughly on the top of my head.

And then he got on his bike and rode away.

CHAPTER

15

Two things happened right after that.

The first was that the bell rang. The second was that Karen Sue Hankey, who had seen the whole thing, went, in her shrill voice, "Oh, my God, Jess. Let a Grit kiss you, why don't you?"

Fortunately for Karen Sue—and for me, I guess—Todd Mintz was standing nearby. So when I dove at her—which I did immediately, of course—with the intention of gouging her eyes out with my thumbs, Todd caught me in midair, swung me around, and said, "Whoa there, tiger."

"Let go of me," I said, red-hot anger replacing the joy that had, just moments before, been coursing through me, causing me to suspect that my heart might explode. "Seriously, Todd, let me go."

"Yeah, let her go, Todd," Karen Sue called. She had dashed up the steps to the main building, and knew she was a safe enough distance away that even if Todd did let go of me—which he didn't seem to have any intention of doing—I'd never catch up to her before she'd ducked into the safety of the building. "I could use another five thousand bucks."

"I bet you could!" I roared. "You could take it and go buy yourself a freaking clue!"

Only I didn't say freaking.

"Oh, very nice," Karen Sue called down from the top of the steps. "Exactly the kind of language I'd expect from a girl whose brother is a murder suspect."

I froze, conscious of the fact that everyone around us was ducking for cover. Or maybe they were just going off to class. It was hard to tell.

"What," I asked, as Todd, sensing from my paralysis that I was no longer a threat to anyone, put me down again, "is she talking about?"

Todd, a big guy in a crew cut who looked as if he wished he were just about anywhere than where, in fact, he was, shrugged.

"I don't know, Jess," he said uncomfortably. "There's just this rumor going around—"

"What rumor?" I demanded.

Todd shifted his weight. "I, um, gotta get to class. I'm gonna be late."

"You tell me what freaking rumor," I snapped, "or I guarantee, you'll be crawling to class on your hands and knees."

Only again, I didn't say freaking.

Todd didn't look scared, though. He just looked tired.

"Look, Jess," he said. "It's just a rumor, okay? Jenna Gibbon's older sister is married to a deputy sheriff with the county, and she said he told her that it looked like they might bring your brother in for questioning, because he fits some kind of profile, and because he doesn't have an alibi for either of the times the attacks occurred. Okay?"

I couldn't believe it. I really couldn't believe it.

Because they'd done it again. Special Agents Johnson and Smith, I mean. They'd said they were going to, and, by God, they had.

Well, and why not? They were with the FBI. They could do anything, right? I mean, who was going to stop them?

One person. Me.

I just couldn't figure out how. I fumed about it for the rest of the day, causing more than one teacher to ask me if perhaps I wouldn't be happier sitting in the guidance office for the rest of the day.

I told them I would—at least there, I figured, I would be free of annoying questions like what's the square root of sixteen hundred and five, what's the pluperfect for *avoir*—but unfortunately, none of them followed through with their threat. When the bell rang at three, I was still free as a bird. Free enough to go stalking past Mark Leskowski, on my way to Ruth's car, without so much as a second glance.

"Jess," he called after me. "Hey, Jess!"

I turned at the sound of my name, and was

mildly surprised to see Mark leave his car, which he'd been unlocking, and hurry up to me.

"Hey," he said. He had on a pair of Ray Bans, which he lifted as he looked down at me. "How are you? I was hoping I'd run into you. I hope I didn't get you into trouble last night."

I just blinked up at him. All I could think about was how, at any minute, the Feds might be hauling Douglas in for questioning about a couple of crimes he in no way could have committed.

If, that is, I didn't come clean about the ESP thing, and promise to help them find their stupid criminals.

"You know," Mark said, I guess judging from my blank expression that I didn't know what he was talking about. "When I dropped you off. Your parents looked kind of . . . mad."

"They weren't mad," I said. "They were concerned." And about Douglas, not me. Because Douglas hadn't been home. He had been off somewhere, alone. . . .

"Oh," Mark said. "Well, anyway. I just wanted to make sure you were, you know, all right. That was pretty terrific, how you found Heather and all."

"Yeah," I said, noticing Ruth coming toward us. "Well, you know. Just doing my job, and all. Listen, I gotta—"

"I was thinking," Mark said, "that maybe if you aren't doing anything this weekend, you and I could, uh, I don't know, hang out."

"Yeah, whatever," I said, though truthfully, the thought of going to see Japanese anime with Skip was a lot more appealing than "uh, I don't know, hanging out" with Mark. "Why don't you give me a call?"

"I'll do that," Mark said. He waved at Ruth as she went by, studying us so intently she nearly barked her shins on her own car's bumper. "Hey," he said to her. "How you doing there?"

"Fine," Ruth said, unlocking the driver's door to her car. "Thanks."

Mark opened his own driver's side door, reached inside his car, and pulled out a duffel bag. Then he closed the door again and locked it. At our glances, which I suppose he perceived as curious—though in my case, it was merely glazed—he went, "Football practice," then shouldered the bag, and headed off in the direction of the gym.

"Jess," Ruth said when he was out of earshot. "Did I hear that correctly? Did Mark Leskowski just ask you out?"

"Yeah," I said.

"So that's how many people who've asked you out today? Two?"

"Yeah," I said, climbing into the passenger seat after she unlocked it from the inside.

"Jeez, Jess," she said. "That's like a record, or something. Why aren't you happier?"

"Because," I said, "one of the guys who asked me out today was, up until recently, a suspect in his own girlfriend's murder, and the other one is your brother."

Ruth went, "Yeah, but isn't Mark off the hook now, on account of what happened to Heather?"

"I guess so," I said. "But. . . ."

"But what?" Ruth asked.

"But . . . Ruth, Tisha says they all knew about that house. Almost like . . . they're the ones who hang out there."

"Meaning?"

"Meaning it must have been one of them."

"One of who?"

"The in crowd," I said, gesturing toward the football field, where we could see the cheerleaders and some of the players already out there, practicing.

"Not necessarily," Ruth said. "I mean, Tisha knew about the house. She didn't say she'd ever been in there partying, did she?"

"Well," I said. "No. Not exactly. But—"

"I mean, come on. Don't you think those guys could find a nicer place to party? Like Mark Leskowski's parents' rec room, for instance? I mean, I hear the Leskowskis have an indoor/outdoor pool."

"Maybe Mr. and Mrs. Leskowski disapprove of Mark's friends bringing their girlfriends over for a quickie in their rec room."

"Puh-lease," Ruth said as we cruised out of the parking lot and turned onto High School Road. "Why would any of them kill Amber? Or try to kill Heather? They're all friends, right?"

Right. Ruth was right. Ruth was always right. And I was always wrong. Well, almost always, anyway.

I guess I didn't really believe—in spite of what Tisha had told me, about all of them knowing about the house on the pit road—that they'd actually been involved in Amber's murder and Heather's attack. I mean, seriously: Mark Leskowski, wrapping his hands around his girlfriend's neck and strangling her? No way. He'd loved her. He'd cried in the guidance office in front of me, he'd loved her so much.

At least, I think that's why he'd been crying. He certainly hadn't been crying about his chances at winning a scholarship being endangered by his status as a murder suspect. I mean, that would have been just plain cold. Right?

And what about Heather? Did I suppose that Jeff Day or someone else on the team had tied Heather up and left her in that bathtub to die? Why? So she wouldn't narc on Mark?

No. It was ridiculous. Tisha's theory about the deranged hillbillies made more sense. Maybe the cheerleaders and the football team partied in the house on the pit road, but they weren't the ones who'd left Heather there. No, that had been the work of someone else. Some sick, perverted individual.

But not—absolutely not—my brother.

I made sure of that, the second I got home. Not, of course, that I'd had any reason to doubt it. I just wanted to set the record straight. I stalked up the stairs—my mother wasn't home, thank God, so I didn't have to listen to any more lectures about how unsuitable it was of me to sneak out in the middle of the night with a boy who worked in a garage—and banged once on Douglas's bedroom door. Then I threw it open, because Douglas's bedroom door doesn't have a lock. My dad took the lock off, after he slit his wrists in there and we had to break the door down to get to him.

He's so used to me barging in, he doesn't even look up anymore.

"Get out," he said, without lifting his gaze from the copy of *Starship Troopers* he was perusing.

"Douglas," I said. "I have to know. Where were you last night from five o'clock until eight, when you came back to the house?"

He looked up at that. "Why do I have to tell you?" he wanted to know.

"Because," I said.

I wanted to tell him the truth, of course. I wanted to say, Douglas, the Feds think you may have had something to do with Amber Mackey's murder, and Heather Montrose's attack. I need you to tell me you didn't do it. I need you to tell me that you have witnesses who can verify your whereabouts at the time these crimes occurred, and that your alibi is rock solid. Because unless you can tell me these things, I may have to take an after-school job working with some particularly nasty people.

In other words, the FBI.

But I wasn't sure I could say these things to Douglas. I wasn't sure I could say these things to Douglas because it was hard to tell anymore what might set off one of his episodes. Most of the time, he seemed normal to me. But every once in a while, something would upset him— something seemingly stupid, like that we were out of Cheerios—and suddenly the voices— Douglas's voices—were back.

On the other hand, this was something serious. It wasn't about Cheerios or reporters from *Good Housekeeping* magazine standing in our yard wanting to interview me. Not this time. This time, it was about people dying.

"Douglas," I said. "I mean it. I need to know where you were. There's this rumor going around—I don't believe it or anything—but there's this rumor going around that you killed Amber Mackey, and that last night you kidnapped Heather Montrose and left her to die."

"Whoa." Douglas, who was lying on his bed, put down his comic book. "And how did I do this, supposedly? Using my superpowers?"

"No," I said. "I think the theory is that you snapped."

"I see," Douglas said. "And who is promoting this theory?"

"Well," I said, "Karen Sue Hankey in particular, but also most of the junior class of Ernie Pyle High, along with some of the seniors, and, um, oh, yeah, the Federal Bureau of Investigation."

"Hmmm." Douglas considered this. "I find that last part particularly troubling. Does the FBI have proof or something that I killed these girls?"

"It's just one girl that's dead," I said. "The other one just got beat up."

"Well, why can't they ask her who beat her up?" Douglas wanted to know. "I mean, she'll tell them it wasn't me."

"She doesn't know who did it," I said. "She said they wore masks. And I figure even if she did know, she's not going to say. I am assuming whoever did this to her told her he'd finish the job if she talked."

Douglas sat up. "You're serious," he said. "People really do suspect me of doing this?"

"Yeah," I said. "And the thing is, the Feds are saying that unless I, you know, become a junior G-man, they're going to pin this thing on you. So before I sign up for my pension plan, I need to know. Have you got any kind of alibi at all?"

Douglas blinked at me. His eyes, like mine, were brown.

"I thought," he said, "that you'd told them you lost your psychic abilities."

"I did," I said. "I think my finding Heather Montrose in the middle of nowhere last night kind of tipped them off that maybe I hadn't been completely up front with them on that particular subject."

"Oh." Douglas looked uncomfortable. "The thing is, what I was doing last night . . . and the night that other girl disappeared . . . well, I was sort of hoping nobody would find out."

I stared at him. My God! So he *had* been up to something! But not, surely, lying in wait at that house on the pit road for an innocent cheerleader to go strolling by. . . .

"Douglas," I said. "I don't care what you were

doing, so long as it didn't involve anything illegal. I just need something—preferably the truth—to tell Allan and Jill, or my butt is going to have 'Property of the U.S. Government' on it for the foreseeable future. So long as they have something on you, they own me. So I have to know. Do they have something on you?"

"Well," Douglas said, slowly. "Sort of. . . ."

I could feel my world tilting, slowly . . . so slowly . . . right off its axis. My brother, Douglas. My big brother Douglas, whom all my life, it seemed, I'd been defending from others, people who called him retard, and spaz, and dorkus. People who wouldn't sit near him when we went to the movies as kids because sometimes he shouted things—that usually didn't make sense to everyone else—at the screen. People who wouldn't let their kids swim in the pool near him, because sometimes Douglas simply stopped swimming and just sank to the bottom, until a lifeguard noticed and fished him out. People who, every time a bike, or a dog, or a plaster yard gnome disappeared from the neighborhood, accused Douglas of having been the one who'd taken it, because Douglas . . . well, he wasn't all there, was he?

Only of course they were wrong. Douglas *was* all there. Just not in the way *they* considered normal.

But maybe, all this time . . . maybe they'd been right. Maybe this time Douglas really had done something wrong. Something so wrong, he didn't even want to tell me about it. *Me*, his kid sister, the one who'd learned how to swing a punch when she turned seven, just so that she could knock the blocks off the kids down the street who were calling him a freakazoid every time he passed by their house on the way to school.

"Douglas," I breathed, finding that my throat had suddenly, and inexplicably, closed. "What did you do?"

"Well," he said, unable to meet my gaze. "The truth is, Jess . . . the truth is . . ." He took a deep breath.

"I got a job."

CHAPTER

16

The first call came right after dinner.

It was a quiet affair, dinner that night. Quiet because every single person at the table was angry with somebody else.

My mother, of course, was angry at me for having snuck out the night before with Rob Wilkins, a boy of whom she did not approve because a) he was too old for me, b) he had no aspirations for attending college, c) he rode a motorcycle, d) his mother was a waitress, and e) we did not know who Mr. Wilkins was or what he did, if anything, or if there even *was* a Mr. Wilkins, which Mary Wilkins had never admitted either way, at least in the presence of my father.

And she didn't even know about the whole probation thing.

My father was mad at my mother for being what he called an elitist snob and for not being more grateful that Rob had insisted on accompanying me on another of what he referred to as my idiotic vision quests, and making sure I didn't get myself killed.

I was mad at my dad for calling my psychic visions idiotic, when they had, as a matter of fact, saved a lot of lives and reunited a lot of families. I was also mad at him for thinking that, without some guy to watch over me, I could not take care of myself. And of course I was mad at my mom for not liking Rob.

Meanwhile, Douglas was mad at me because I had told him he had to 'fess up to Mom and Dad about the job thing. I fully understood why he didn't want to—Mom was going to flip out at the idea of her baby boy soiling his fingers at any sort of menial labor. She seemed to be convinced that the slightest provocation—like him maybe lifting a sponge to wipe the milk he'd spilled on the kitchen counter—was going to set him off into another suicidal tailspin.

But Dad was the one who was really going to bust a gut when he found out, and I don't mean from laughing, either. In our family, if you worked, you worked at one of Dad's restaurants, or not at all. That whole thing where they'd let me spend the summer as a camp counselor? Yeah, that had only come about because of the intensive musical training I would be receiving while I was at Wawasee. Otherwise, you can bet I'd have been relegated to the steam table at Joe's.

So I wasn't too happy with Mom, Dad, or

Douglas during that particular meal, and none of them were too happy with me, either. So when the phone rang, you can bet I ran for it, just as a way to avoid the uncomfortable silence that had hung over the table, interrupted only by the occasional scraping fork, or request for more parmesan.

"Hello?" I said, snatching up the receiver from the kitchen wall phone, which was the closest one to the dining room.

"Jess Mastriani?" a male voice asked.

"Yes," I said, with some surprise. I had expected it to be Ruth. She's about the only person who ever calls us. I mean, unless something is wrong at one of the restaurants. "This is she."

"I saw you talking to Tisha Murray today," the person on the other end of the phone said.

"Uh," I said. "Yeah." The voice sounded weird. Sort of muffled, like whoever it was was calling from inside a tunnel or something. "So?"

"So if you do it again," the voice said, "you're going to end up just like Amber Mackey."

I took the receiver away from my ear and looked down at it, just like they always do in horror movies when the psychopathic killer calls (generally from inside the house). I've always thought that was stupid, because it's not like you can see the person through the phone. But you know, it must be instinctive or something, because there I was, doing it.

I put the phone back up to my ear and went, "You're kidding me with this, right?"

"Stop asking questions about the house on the pit road," the voice said. "Or you'll be sorry, you stupid bitch."

"What are you going to do," I asked, "when I hang up and star-six-nine you, and five minutes later, the cops show up and haul your ass into jail, you freaking perv?"

The line went dead in my ear. I banged down the receiver and pushed the star button, then the number six, then the number nine. A phone rang, and then a woman's voice said, "The number you are trying to call cannot be reached by this method."

Damn! They'd called from an untraceable line. I should have known.

I hung up and went back into the dining room.

"I wish Ruth would stop calling us during dinner," my mother said. "She knows we eat at six thirty. It really isn't very thoughtful of her."

I didn't see any reason to disabuse her of the idea that it had been Ruth on the phone. I was pretty sure she wouldn't have liked hearing the truth. I plunked down into my seat and picked up my fork.

Only suddenly, I couldn't eat. I don't know what happened, but I had a piece of pasta halfway to my lips when suddenly my throat closed up and the table—and all of the food on it— went blurry.

Blurry because my eyes had filled up with tears. Tears! Just like Mark Leskowski, I was crying.

"Jess," my mother said, curiously. "Are you all right?"

I glanced at her, but I couldn't really see her. Nor could I speak. All I could think was, *Oh, my God. They are going to do to me what they did to Heather.*

And then I felt really, really cold, like someone had left the door to the walk-in freezer at Mastriani's wide open.

"Jessica?" my dad said. "What's wrong?"

But how could I tell them? How could I tell them about that phone call? It would just upset them. They would probably even call the police. That was all I needed, the police. Like I didn't have the FBI practically camped in my front yard.

But Heather . . . what had happened to Heather . . . I didn't want that to happen to me.

Suddenly Douglas shoved his salad plate to the floor. It shattered with a crash into a million pieces.

"Take that," he yelled at the bits of lettuce with ranch dressing littering the floor.

I blinked at him through my tears. What was going on? Was Douglas having an episode? I could tell by the expressions on my parents' faces that they thought so, anyway. They exchanged worried glances. . . .

And while their attention was focused on one another, Douglas glanced at me, and winked. . . .

A second later, my mother was on her feet. "Dougie," she cried. "Dougie, what is it?"

My dad, as always, was more laconic about the whole thing. "Did you take all your medication today, Douglas?" he asked.

Then I knew. Douglas was faking an episode—to get them off my back about the crying thing. I felt a wave of love for Douglas wash over me. Had there ever, in the history of time, been such a cool big brother?

While my parents were distracted, I reached up and wiped the tears from my eyes with the backs of my wrists. What was happening to me? I never cried. This thing with Amber, and now with Heather, was getting way personal. I mean, now they were after me. Me!

Between the Feds thinking Douglas was the killer, and the real killers threatening that I was going to be their next victim, I guess I had a reason to cry. But it was still demoralizing, seeing as how it was such a Karen-Sue-Hankey thing to do.

While I was trying to get my emotions under control, and my parents were questioning Douglas about his mental health, the phone rang again. This time, I practically knocked my chair over, diving to get it.

"It's for me," I said quickly, lifting the receiver. "I'm sure."

No one so much as glanced in my direction. Douglas was still getting the third degree for his assault on his dinner salad.

"Jessica?" a voice I did not recognize asked in my ear.

"It's me," I said. And then, turning my back on the scene in the dining room, I said in a low rapid voice, "Listen, you loser, if you don't quit calling me, I swear I'm going to hunt you down and kill you like the dog that you are."

The voice went, sounding extremely taken aback, "But, Jess. This is the first time I've called you. Ever."

I sucked in my breath, finally realizing who it was. *"Skip?"*

"Yeah," Skip said. "It's me. Listen, I was just wondering if you'd thought about what we discussed today at lunch. You know. The movie. This weekend."

"Oh," I said. My mother came into the kitchen and went to the pantry, from which she removed a broom and dustpan. "Yeah," I said. "The movie. This weekend."

"Yeah," Skip said. "And I thought maybe, before the movie, we could go out. You know, for dinner or something."

"Uh," I said. My mother, holding the broom and dustpan, was standing there staring at me, the way lions on the Discovery Channel stare at the gazelles they are about to pounce on. All her concern for Douglas seemed to be forgotten. This was, after all, the first time I had ever been asked out within her earshot. My mother, who'd been a cheerleader herself—and Homecoming Queen, Prom Queen, County Fair Princess, and Little Miss Corn Detassler—had been waiting sixteen years for me to start dating. She blamed the fact that I hadn't been out on a million dates already, like she had at my age, on my slovenly dress habits.

She didn't know anything about my right hook.

Well, actually, I think she did now, thanks to Mrs. Hankey's lawsuit.

"Yeah, about that, Skip," I said, turning my back on her. "I don't think I can go. I mean, my curfew is eleven. My mom would never let me stay out for a movie that didn't even start until midnight."

"Yes, I would," my mother said loudly, to my utter horror and disbelief.

I brought the phone away from my ear and stared at her. "Mom," I said, flabbergasted.

"Don't look at me that way, Jessica," my mom said. "I mean, I am not completely inflexible. If you want to go to a midnight show with Skip, that's perfectly all right."

I couldn't believe it. After the grief she'd been giving me about Rob, I was pretty sure she was never letting me out of the house again, let alone with a boy.

But apparently it was just one particular boy I was banned from seeing socially.

And that boy was not Skip Abramowitz.

"I mean," my mother went on, "it's not like your father and I don't know Skip. He has grown into a very responsible young man. Of course you can go to the movies with him."

I gaped at her. "Ma," I said. "The movie doesn't even start until midnight."

"So long as Skip has you home right after it ends," my mother said.

"Oh," came a voice from the receiver, which I was holding limply in my hand. "I will, Mrs. Mastriani. Don't worry!"

And just like that, I had a date with Skip Abramowitz.

Well, it wasn't like I could get out of it after that. Not without completely humiliating him. Or myself, for that matter.

"Mom," I yelled when I had hung up. "I don't want to go out with Skip!"

"Why not?" Mom wanted to know. "I think he's a very nice boy."

Translation: He doesn't own a motorcycle, has never worked in a garage, and did really well on his PSATs.

And, oh, yeah, his dad happens to be the highest-paid lawyer in town.

"I think you're being unfair, Jessica," my mother said. "True, Skip may not be the most exciting boy you know, but he's extremely sweet."

"Sweet! He blew up my favorite Barbie!"

"That was years ago," my mom said. "I think Skip's grown into a real gentleman. You two will have a wonderful time." She grew thoughtful. "You know, I just found a skirt pattern the other day that would be perfect for a casual night out at the movies. And there are a few yards of gingham left over from those curtains I made for the guest room. . . ."

See, this is the problem with having a stay-at-home mom. She thinks up little projects to do all the time, like making me a skirt from material left over from curtains. I swear sometimes I'm not sure who she's supposed to be, my mother or Maria von Trapp.

Before I could say anything like, "No, thanks, Mom. I just spent a fortune at Esprit, I think I can manage to find something to wear on my own," or even, "Mom, if you think I'm not planning on coming down with something Saturday night just before this date, you've got another think coming," Douglas came into the kitchen, holding his dinner plate, and said, "Yeah, Jess. Skip's really neat."

I shot him a warning look. "Watch it, Comic-Book Boy," I growled.

Douglas, looking alarmed, noticed Mom standing there with the broom. "Oh, hey," he said, putting his empty dinner plate down in the sink. "I'll clean it up, don't worry. It was my fault, anyway."

My mom snatched the broom out of his reach. "No, no," she said, hurrying back into the dining room. "I'll do it."

Which was kind of sad. Because of course she was only doing it because she didn't want Douglas messing with bits of broken glass. His suicide attempt last Christmas had convinced her that he wasn't to be trusted around sharp objects.

"See," Douglas said, as the swinging door closed behind her, "what I go through for you? Now she's going to be watching me like a hawk for the next few days."

I suppose I should have been grateful to him. But all I could think was that things would be a lot less stressful if Douglas would just come clean.

"Why don't you go tell them now?" I asked. All right, begged. "Before *Entertainment Tonight.* You know Mom never lets a fight last more than five minutes into *ET.*"

Douglas was rinsing his plate.

"No way," he said, not looking at me.

I nearly burst a capillary, I was so mad.

"Douglas," I hissed. "If you think I'm not telling the Feds, you're out of your mind. I can't let them go around thinking they have something on me. I'm telling them. And if they know, how long do you think it's going to be before Mom and Dad find out? It's better for *you* to tell them than the damned FBI, don't you think?"

Douglas turned the water off.

"It's just that you know what Dad's going to say," he said. "If I'm well enough to work behind the counter at the comic book store, I'm well enough to work in the kitchens at Mastriani's. But I can't stand food service. You know that."

"Who can?" I wanted to know. But when your dad owned three of the most popular restaurants in town, you didn't have much of a choice.

"And Mom." Douglas shook his head. "You know how Mom's going to react. That out there? That was nothing."

"That's why I'd tell them now," I said, "before they find out from somebody else. I mean, for God's sake, Douglas. You've been working there for two weeks already. You think they aren't going to hear about it from somebody?"

"Look, Jess," Douglas said. "I'll tell them. I swear I will. Just let me do it my own way, in my own time. I mean, you know how Mom is—"

The swinging door to the dining room banged open, and my mother, carrying the now full dustpan, came into the kitchen.

"You know how Mom is what?" she asked, looking suspiciously from Douglas to me and then back again.

Fortunately, the phone rang.

Again.

I leapt for it, but I was too late. My dad had already picked up the extension in the den.

"Jess," he yelled. "Phone for you."

Great. My mother's eyes lit up. You could totally tell that she thought it was starting for me. You know, the popularity that she had had when she was my age, which had so far eluded me during my tenure at Ernie Pyle High. As a daughter I was, I knew, pretty disappointing to her, because I wasn't already going steady with a guy like Mark Leskowski. I guess at this point, even a date with Skip was preferable to no date at all.

Or Rob.

Too bad she didn't know that the kind of calls I'd been receiving all night were not exactly from members of the pep squad, wanting to discuss the next day's bake sale.

No, more like members of the death squad, wanting to discuss my imminent demise.

But when I picked up, I found that it wasn't

my prank caller at all. It was Special Agent Johnson.

"Well, Jessica," he said. "Have you given any thought to our conversation this morning?"

I looked at my mom and Douglas. "Uh, do you guys mind?" I asked. "This is kind of personal."

My mom's eyebrows furrowed. "It isn't that boy, is it?" she wanted to know. "That Wilkins person?"

That Wilkins person. It was almost as bad as the Jerk.

"No," I said. "It's another boy."

Which wasn't technically even a lie. And which made my mom smile as happily as she left the room as if I'd just been voted Most Likely to Marry a Doctor. Douglas left too, only he didn't look half so happy as Mom did.

"Which conversation?" I asked Special Agent Johnson, as soon as my mother was gone. "Oh, you mean the one where you suggested my brother might, in fact, be Amber Mackey's killer? And that if I didn't help you track down your little Ten Most Wanteds, you'd haul him in for questioning about it?"

"Well, I don't think I put it quite like that," Special Agent Johnson said. "But that, in essence, is why I'm calling."

"I hate to break it to you," I said, "but Douglas has got a rock solid alibi for the times both those girls disappeared. Just ask his new employers down at Comix Underground."

There was silence on the line. Then Special Agent Johnson chuckled.

"I was wondering," he said, "how long it would take for him to work up the courage to tell you."

I felt a jolt of rage. *You knew?* I was going to scream into the receiver.

But then it hit me. Of course he'd known. He and his partner had known all along. They'd just been using the fact that I didn't know to yank my chain.

Well, that's what they get paid for. Covert operations.

"If you're done having your little fun with me," I said—with more irritation than was perhaps necessary, but I felt tears threatening again—"you might actually want to do some work for a change. I mean, I know it's more fun for you all to try to get me to do your job for you, but in this particular case, I think you've got the expertise."

I told him about my mysterious caller. Special Agent Johnson was, I must say, mightily interested.

"And you say you didn't recognize the voice?" he asked.

"Well," I said. "It sounded kind of muffled."

"He probably put something over the mouthpiece of the phone he was using," Special Agent Johnson said, "for fear you might recognize him. Let me ask you something. Was the voice distinctive in any way? Any accents, or anything?"

For some reason, I found myself remembering the Grit Test. You know, the pen versus pin thing.

"No," I said, with some surprise at myself for not having realized it before. "No accent at all."

"Good," Special Agent Johnson said. "Good girl. All right, we'll work on seeing if we can come up with the number this person called from."

"Well, I would think you should be able to come up with that pretty easily," I said. "Seeing as how you've had my phone tapped since like, forever."

"That's very funny, Jessica," Special Agent Johnson said, dryly. "You are aware, of course, that the Bureau would never do anything to violate a U.S. citizen's rights during an investigation."

"Haw," I said. Somehow, knowing Special Agent Johnson was on the case made me feel better. Crazy, huh, considering how much having the Feds following me around all the time used to bug me? "Haw, haw."

"And don't worry, Jessica," Special Agent Johnson said. "You and your family are in no danger. We'll post plenty of operatives outside your home tonight."

Too bad that isn't what they chose to destroy in order to assure me of how serious they were about their threats. Our home, I mean.

Instead, they burned down Mastriani's.

CHAPTER

17

You'd have thought I'd be able to catch a break, wouldn't you? I mean, it wasn't like I'd gotten any sleep the night before. No, they had to make sure I didn't get any the next night, either.

Well, okay, I got *some.* The call didn't come until after three.

Three in the morning, I mean.

But when it did come, there was no sleep for anyone in the Mastriani household. Not for a long, long time.

I, of course, thought it was for me.

And why not? It wasn't like the phone had rung—not even once that night—for anybody else in the house. No, all of my mother's dreams for me were finally coming true: I was Miss Popularity, all right.

Too bad the only dates I was getting were dates with, um, death.

Well, and Skip Abramowitz.

When the phone started ringing its head off at three A.M., I shot out of bed before I was even fully awake and dove for the extension in my room, as if somehow, by catching it on the second ring, I was going to keep the rest of the house from waking up.

Yeah, nice try.

The voice on the other end of the line was familiar, but it wasn't one of my new friends. You know, the ones who'd promised to kill me if I talked to Tisha Murray anymore about the house on the pit road.

It was, instead, a woman's voice. It took me a minute to realize it was Special Agent Smith.

"Jessica," she said when I answered. And then, when my dad got on the line in his bedroom, and went, blearily, "Hullo?" she added, "Mr. Mastriani."

My dad and I didn't say anything. He, I think, was still trying to wake up. I, of course, was tensing for what I knew was going to follow . . . or thought I knew, anyway. Someone else was missing. Tisha Murray, maybe.

Or Heather Montrose. Despite the guard they'd put on her room in the hospital, someone had managed to sneak in, and finish the job they'd started. Heather was dead.

Either that, or they'd found someone. They'd found someone trying to sneak into my house to kill me.

But of course it wasn't that at all. It wasn't any of those things.

"I'm sorry to wake you, sir," Jill said, sounding as if she meant it. "But I think you should know that your restaurant, Mastriani's, is on fire. Could you please—"

But Jill never got to finish, because my dad had dropped the phone and was, if I knew him, already reaching for his pants.

"We'll be right there," I said.

"No, Jessica, not you. You should—"

But I never found out what I have should have done, because I'd hung up.

When I met him at the front door a few seconds later, I saw that I'd been right. My dad was fully dressed—well, he had on pants and shoes. He was still wearing his pajama top as a shirt. When he saw me, he said, "Stay here with your mother and brother."

I, however, had gotten dressed, too.

"No way," I said.

He looked annoyed but grateful at the same time, which was quite a feat, if you think about it.

As soon as we stepped outside, we could see it. An orange glow reflected against the low hanging clouds in the night sky. And not a small glow, either, but something that looked like that burning-of-Atlanta scene out of *Gone With the Wind*.

"Christ almighty," my dad said when he saw it.

I, of course, was busy consulting with my friends across the street. The ones in the white van.

"Hey," I said, tapping on the rolled up window on the driver's side. "I gotta go downtown with my dad. Stay here and keep an eye on the place while I'm gone, okay?"

There was no response, but I hadn't expected any. People who are supposed to be covertly following you don't like it when you come up and start talking to them, even if their boss knows that you know they're there.

Well, you know what I mean.

The drive downtown took no time at all. At least, it didn't usually. And yet it seemed to take ages that night. Our house is only a few blocks from downtown . . . a fifteen-minute stroll, at most, a four-minute drive. The streets, at three in the morning, were empty. That wasn't the problem. It was that orange glow hanging in the sky above our heads that we couldn't take our eyes off of. A couple of times, my dad nearly drove off the side of the road, he was so transfixed by it. It was a good thing, actually, that I was there, since I'd taken the wheel and gone, "Dad."

"Don't worry," I said to him, a minute later. "That isn't it. That orange light? That's probably, you know, heat lightning."

"Staying in one place?" my dad asked.

"Sure," I said. "I read about it. In Bio."

God, I am such a liar.

And then we turned the corner onto Main. And there it was.

And it wasn't heat lightning. Oh, no.

Once, a long time ago, the people who lived across the street from us had a log roll out of their fireplace and set the living room curtains on fire.

That was how I'd expected the fire at Mastriani's to be. You know, flames in the windows, and maybe some smoke billowing out of the open front door. The fire department would be there, of course, and they'd put the flames out, and that would be the end of it. That's what had happened with our neighbors. Their curtains were lost, and the carpet had to be replaced, along with a couch that had gotten completely soaked by the fire hoses.

But you know that night—the night the curtains caught fire—the people who lived across the street slept in their own—somewhat smoky-smelling—beds. They hadn't needed to go stay with relatives or in a shelter or a hotel or anything, because of course their house was still standing.

The fire at Mastriani's was not that kind of fire. It was not that kind of fire at all. The fire at Mastriani's was a writhing, breathing, living thing. It was, to put it mildly, awesome in its destructive power. Flames were shooting thirty, forty feet in the air from the roof. The entire building was a glowing ball of fire. We couldn't get closer than two hundred feet away from it, there were so many fire engines parked along the street. Dozens of firefighters, wielding hoses spitting streams of water, weaved a dreamy, dance-like pattern in front of the building, trying to douse the flames.

But it was a losing battle. You did not need to be a fire marshall to tell that. The place was engulfed, consumed in flames. It was not even recognizable anymore. The green and gold awning above the door, that shielded customers from the rain? Gone. The matching green sign, with MASTRIANI'S spelled out across it in gold script? Gone. The window boxes on the second floor administrative offices? Gone. The new industrial freezers? Gone. The make-out table where Mark Leskowski and I had sat? Gone. Everything, gone.

Just like that.

Well, not just like that, actually. Because as my dad and I got out of the car and picked our way toward the place, carefully stepping over the hoses that, pulsing like live snakes, crisscrossed the road, we could see that a lot of people were working very hard to save what appeared to me, anyway, to be a lost cause. Firefighters shouted above the hiss of water and the roar of the flame, coughing in the thick, black smoke that instantly clogged the throat and lungs.

One of them noticed us and said to stand back. My dad yelled, "I own the place," and the firefighter directed us to a group of people who were standing across the street, their faces bathed in orange light.

"Joe," one of them yelled, and I recognized him as the mayor of our town, which is small. If there were going to be a catastrophic fire threatening not only one prominent downtown business, but the businesses around it as well, you would expect the mayor to be there.

"Jesus, Joe," the mayor said. "I'm sorry."

"Was anybody hurt?" my dad asked, coming to stand between the mayor and a man I knew from his periodic inspections to be the fire chief. "Nobody's been hurt, have they?"

"Naw," the mayor said. "Coupla Richie's guys, trying to be heroes, went in to make sure nobody was still inside, and got a chestful of smoke for their efforts."

"They'll be okay," Richard Parks, the fire chief, said. "Nobody was in there, Joe. Don't worry about that."

My dad looked relieved, but only moderately so. "What are the chances of it spreading?" Mastriani's was a freestanding structure, a Victorian-type house flanked on either side by a New Age bookstore and a bank branch, with a shared parking lot behind it. "The bank? Harmony Books?"

"We're watering them down," the fire chief said. "So far, so good. Coupla sparks landed on the roof of the bookstore and went out right away. We got here in time, Joe, don't worry. Well, in time to save the neighboring structures, anyway."

His voice was sorrowful. And why not? He'd eaten at Mastriani's a lot. Just like every single man there, pointing a hose at it.

"What happened?" my dad asked in a stunned voice. "I mean, how did it start? Does anybody know?"

"Couldn't say," Captain Parks told us. "Folks

over at the jailhouse heard an explosion, looked out, saw the place was on fire. Couldn'ta been more than eight, nine minutes ago. Place went up like a cinder."

"Which suggests," a woman's voice said, "an accelerant to me."

We all looked around. And there stood Special Agents Smith and Johnson, looking concerned and maybe a little worse for wear. To be roused from a dead sleep two nights in a row was a little rough, even for them.

"My thinking exactly," the fire chief said.

"Wait a minute." My dad, his face scratchy-looking with a half-night's growth of beard bristle, stared at the FBI agents. "What are you saying? You're saying somebody purposefully started this fire?"

"No way it coulda spread that fast, Joe," the fire chief said, "or burned so hot. Not without some kind of accelerant. From the smell, I'm guessing gasoline, but we won't know until the fire's out and the place has cooled down enough for us to—"

"Gasoline?" My dad looked as if he was about to have a heart attack. Seriously. All these veins I had never noticed before were standing out in his forehead, and his neck looked kind of skinny, like it could barely support the weight of his head.

Or maybe it was just that, in the bright light from the fire, I was getting my first really good look at him in a while.

"Why in God's name would anybody do this?" my dad demanded. "Why would anybody deliberately burn the place down?"

The sheriff, whom I hadn't noticed before, cleared his throat and went, "Disgruntled employee, maybe."

"I haven't fired anybody," my dad said. "Not in months."

That was true. My dad didn't like firing people, so he only hired people he was pretty sure were going to work out. And mostly, his instincts were right on.

"Well," the sheriff said, gazing almost admiringly at the blaze across the street. "There'll be an investigation. That's for sure. Case of arson? You can bet your insurance company'll be all over it. We'll get to the bottom of it. Eventually."

Eventually. Sure. Or they could, I supposed, just have asked me. I'd have been able to tell them who started it. I knew good and well.

Well, actually, what I knew was the why. Not the who. But the why was clear enough.

It was a warning. A warning about what would happen to me if I didn't quit asking questions about the house on the pit road.

Which was so unfair. My dad. My poor dad. He'd done nothing to deserve this, nothing at all.

Looking at him, at his face as he tried to joke with the mayor and the sheriff and the fire chief, my heart swelled with pity. He was joking, but inside, I knew, his heart was breaking. My dad had loved Mastriani's, which he'd opened shortly after he and my mom had married. It had been his first restaurant, his first baby . . . just like Douglas was Mom's first baby. And now that baby was going up in a puff of smoke.

Well, not really a puff, actually. More like a wall. A great big wall of smoke that would soon be floating across the county like a storm cloud.

"Don't even think about it, Jess," Special Agent Johnson said, not without some affability.

I turned to blink at him. "Think about what?"

"Finding out who did this," Allan said, "and going after them yourself. We're talking about some dangerous—and fairly sick—criminals here. You leave the investigating to us, understand?"

For once, I was perfectly willing to do so. I mean, I was mad and everything. Don't get me wrong. But a part of me was also scared. More scared even than I'd been when I'd seen Heather all tied up in that bathtub. More scared than I'd been on that motorcycle, careening through the darkness of those woods.

Because this—the fire—was more terrible, in a way, than either of those things. This was awful, more awful than Heather's broken arm, and way more awful than me tipping over beneath an eight-hundred-pound bike.

Because this . . . this was out of control. This was dangerous. This was deadly.

Like what had happened to Amber.

"Don't worry," I said, gulping. "I will."

"Yeah," Special Agent Johnson said, clearly not believing me. "Right."

And then I heard it. My mom's voice, calling out my dad's name.

She came toward us, picking her way through the fire hoses, with a trench coat thrown over her nightgown and Douglas holding onto her elbow to keep her from tripping in her high-heeled sandals. My dad, seeing her, started forward, meeting her just beside one of the biggest fire engines.

"Oh, Joe," my mom said, sighing as she watched the flames that still seemed to rise so high into the sky, they were practically licking it. "Oh, Joe."

"It's all right, Toni," my dad said, taking her hand. "I mean, don't worry. The insurance is all paid up. We're totally covered. We can rebuild."

"But all that work, Joe," my mom said. Her gaze never left the fire, as if it had transfixed her. And you know, even though it was this horrible thing, it was still beautiful, in a way. The fire-fighters had given up trying to put the flames out, and were instead concentrating on keeping them from spreading to the buildings next door. And so far, they were doing a good job.

"All your hard work. Twenty years of it." I saw my mom tilt her head until it was resting on my dad's shoulder. "I'm so sorry, Joe."

"It's okay," my dad said. He let go of her hand, and put his arm around her instead. "It's just a restaurant. That's all. Just a restaurant."

Just a restaurant. Just my dad's dream restaurant, that's all, the one he'd worked hardest and longest on. Joe's, my dad's less-expensive restaurant, brought in barely half the income of

Mastriani's, and Joe Junior's, the take-out pizza place, even less than that. We were, I knew, going to be hurting financially for a while, insurance or no insurance.

But my dad didn't seem to care. He gave my mom a squeeze and said, with only somewhat forced jocularity, "Hey, if something had to go, I'm glad it's this and not the house."

They didn't say anything else after that. They just stood there with their arms around each other and their heads together, watching a big part of their livelihood go up in smoke.

Douglas came up to me. I didn't tell him what I was thinking, which was that the last time I'd seen our parents standing like that, it had been outside the emergency room, when he'd slashed his wrists last Christmas Eve.

"I guess," Douglas said, "now probably wouldn't be a good time to tell them, right?"

I looked at him. "Tell them what?"

"About my new job."

I couldn't help smiling a little at that.

"Uh, no," I said. "Now would definitely not be a good time to tell them about your new job."

And so the four of us stood and watched Mastriani's burn down.

CHAPTER

18

By the time I got to school the next day, it was noon, and everyone—everyone in the entire town—had heard what had happened. When I walked through the doors of the caf—it was my lunch period when Mom dropped me off—all these people came rushing up to me to express their condolences. Really, just like somebody had died.

And, in a way, I guess, somebody *had* died. I mean, Mastriani's was an institution in our town. It was where people went when they wanted to splurge, like on a birthday, or before prom or something.

But I guess not anymore.

I think I've mentioned how extremely not popular I am at my Ernest Pyle High. I mean, I don't have what you would call school spirit. I could really care less if the Cougars win State, or even if they win, period. And I don't think I've ever been invited to a party. You know the ones, where somebody's parents aren't home, so everybody comes over with a keg and trashes the place, like in the movies?

Yeah, I've never been invited to one of those.

So I guess you could say I was pretty surprised by the outpouring of sympathy for my situation from a certain segment of the student population at Ernie Pyle High. Because it wasn't just Ruth and Skip and people from the Orchestra who came up to say they were sorry to hear about what had happened.

No, Todd Mintz came up, and a bunch of the Pompettes, and Tisha Murray and Jeff Day, and even the king of the popular crowd himself, Mark Leskowski.

It was almost enough to take a girl's mind off the fact that there was someone out there who wanted her dead—and who'd see that she got that way, if she came too close to the truth.

"I can't believe it," Mark said, plopping his truly magnificent rear end down on the bench beside me and regarding me with those deep brown eyes. "I mean, we were just *there,* you and I."

"Yeah," I said, uncomfortably aware of the number of envious glances coming my way. After all, with Amber gone, Mark was fair game. I saw more than one cheerleader nudge the girl next to her and point to the two of us, sitting there with our heads so close together at the otherwise empty table.

Of course, they had no way of knowing that my heart belonged—and always would—to another.

"At least nobody was hurt," Mark said. "I mean, could you imagine if it had happened during the dinner rush or something?"

"It would have been hard," I said to him, "for whoever poured gasoline all over the place, to have done so without anybody noticing during the dinner rush."

Mark's dark eyebrows lifted. "You mean somebody did it on *purpose*? But *why*? And *who*?"

"My guess would be whoever killed Amber and then beat up Heather. And they did it as a warning," I said. "To me. To back off."

Mark looked stunned. "God," he said. "That *sucks*."

It was more or less an adequate representation of my feelings on the matter, and so I nodded.

"Yeah," I said. "Doesn't it?"

It was right after that that the bell rang. Mark said, "Hey, listen. Maybe we could get together or something this weekend. I mean, if you're up for it. I'll give you a call."

Okay, I'll admit it. It was kind of cool to have the best-looking guy in school—vice-president of the senior class, quarterback, and all around hottie—say things to me like "I'll give you a call." I mean, don't get me wrong: he was no Rob Wilkins or anything. There was that whole "unacceptable" thing, which was a little, I don't know, militaristic for me.

But hey. He'd asked me out. Twice now. All of a sudden, I had a clue as to how my mom must have felt, when she was in school. You know, Little Miss Corn Detassler and all of that. I could see why she'd been so excited for me when Skip had called. Being popular—well, it's pretty fun.

Or at least it was, up until Karen Sue Hankey came up to me on my way to my locker and went, in her snotty Karen-Sue-Hankey voice, "Missed you at chair auditions this morning."

I froze, one hand on my combination lock. The auditions for chair placement in Orchestra. I had completely forgotten. After all, I had been dealing with some pretty heavy stuff lately . . . threats to my life, and the destruction of a large portion of my family's business. It wasn't any wonder I hadn't been able to keep my schedule straight.

But wait a minute . . . the winds had been scheduled for Thursday.

Which was today.

"I suppose, since you missed them," Karen Sue said, "you'll have to be last chair until next semester's tryouts. Too bad. Mr. Vine is posting the placements after school and I'm betting I'll be—Hey!"

The reason Karen Sue yelled "Hey" is because I pushed her. Not hard or anything. I just had to get somewhere, and fast, and she was in my way.

And that somewhere was the teachers' lounge, where I knew Mr. Vine spent fifth period, decompressing after freshman Orchestra.

I tore down the hall, bumping into people

rushing off to class, and not even saying excuse me. It wasn't fair. It totally wasn't fair. A person with an excused absence like mine—and my absence *was* excused—should be allowed to audition like everybody else, not relegated to last chair just because some psycho had burned her parents' restaurant down.

The thing was, I had totally learned to sight read over the summer. I had had this big plan of blowing Mr. Vine away with my awesome new musical abilities. I didn't want to be first chair or anything, but I definitely deserved third, maybe even second. No way was I going to take last chair. Not lying down, anyway.

I skidded to a halt in front of the door to the teachers' lounge. I was going to be late for Bio, but I didn't care. I banged on the door.

As I was doing so, somebody touched my shoulder. I turned around, and was surprised to see Claire Lippman, who hardly ever spoke to me in the hallways. Not because she was snotty or anything, just because, usually, she had her head buried in a script.

"Jess," she said. Claire did not look good. Which was also unusual, because Claire is one of those, you know, raving beauties. The kind you maybe don't notice right off, but the more you look at her, the more you realize that she is perfect.

She didn't look so perfect just then, though. She'd chewed all the lipstick off her lower lip, and the pink sweater she'd flung around her shoulders—she was wearing a white sleeveless top—was in grave danger of slipping off and landing on the floor.

"Jess, I . . ." Claire looked up and down the hallway. It was clearing out, as people darted into class. "I really need to talk to you."

I could tell something was wrong. Really wrong.

"What's wrong, Claire?" I asked, putting my hand on her arm. "Are you—"

All right. Are you all right. That's what I'd been going to ask her.

Only I never got the chance, because of two things that happened at almost the same time.

The first was that the door to the teachers' lounge opened, and Mr. Lewis, the chemistry teacher, stood there, looking down at me like I was crazy, because of course people aren't supposed to bother teachers when they are in the lounge.

The second thing that happened was that Mark Leskowski emerged from the guidance office, which was across the hall from the teachers' lounge, holding a stack of college applications they'd evidently been keeping there for him.

"What may I do for you, Miss Mastriani?" Mr. Lewis asked. I had never had Chemistry, but he apparently knew my name from last spring, when I'd been in the paper so much.

"Hey," Mark said, to Claire and me. "How you two doing?"

Which was when Claire did an extraordinary

thing. She spun around and took off down the hallway, so fast that she didn't even notice her sweater slip off her shoulders and fall to the carpet.

Mr. Lewis, looking after her, shook his head.

"Drama club," he muttered.

Mark and I—staring after Claire, who disappeared around the corner, heading in the direction of the drama wing, where the auditorium and stuff were—glanced at one another. Mark rolled his eyes and shrugged, as if to say, "Dames. What can you do?"

"See ya," he said, and started off in the opposite direction, toward the gym.

Not knowing what else to do, I bent down and picked up Claire's sweater. It was really soft, and when I glanced at the tag, I saw why. One hundred percent cashmere. She was going to miss this. I'd hang onto it, I decided, until I saw her again.

"Well, Miss Mastriani?" Mr. Lewis said, startling me.

I asked to see Mr. Vine. Mr. Lewis sighed, then went and got him.

Mr. Vine, when he came to the door, seemed to find my concern that I would be relegated to last chair in the flute section very amusing.

"Do you really think," he said, his eyes twinkling, "that I'd do that to you, Jess? We all know why you weren't there. Don't worry about it. Meet me right after last period today and we'll hold your audition. All right?"

I felt relief wash over me. "All right," I said. "Thanks a lot, Mr. Vine."

Shaking his head, Mr. Vine went back into the lounge. When the door closed, I heard him laughing.

But I didn't care. I had my audition. That's all that mattered.

Or at least, that's all that mattered to me, then. But as the day wore on, something else began to nag me.

And it wasn't the same thing that had been nagging me all week, either. I mean, the fact that somebody was going around, attacking cheerleaders, making threatening phone calls to the local psychic, and burning down her parents' restaurant.

No, it was something more than that. It was something I couldn't quite put my finger on.

It wasn't until the middle of seventh period that I realized what it was.

I was scared.

Seriously. I was walking around the hallways of Ernest Pyle High School, feeling frightened out of my mind.

Oh, not like I was a quivering mess, or anything. I wasn't going around, grabbing people and weeping into their shirtfronts.

But I was scared. I was scared about what was happening at home, at my house on Lumley Lane. The Feds were still watching it—heck, they were probably watching me, though I hadn't noticed any tails as I flitted through the hallways.

But that wasn't all. It wasn't just that I was

scared. It was that I knew something was wrong. Something more than just Mastriani's exploding and Amber being dead and Heather hospitalized.

Look, I'm not saying it was a psychic thing. Not at all. Not then.

But there was definitely something not right going on, and it wasn't just that all these things had been happening, and the Feds, so far as I knew, didn't even have a suspect, let alone an arrest. It was more than that. It was . . .

Creepy.

Like the idea of being out a date with Skip. Only much, much worse.

Which was why, midway through seventh period, I couldn't take it anymore. I don't know. I guess I snapped. My hand shot up into the air before I knew what was happening.

And when Mademoiselle MacKenzie, not particularly thrilled to have me interrupt in the middle of our in-depth look at the never-ending battle of wills between Alix and Michel (*Alix mes du sel dans la boule de Michel*), asked, "*Qu'est-ce que vous voulez, Jessica?*" and I went, in English, "I need the hall pass," she made no effort whatsoever to hide her annoyance.

"Can't you wait," she wanted to know, "for the bell?"

It was a logical question, of course. It was two-thirty. Only a half hour of school left.

But the answer was no. No, I couldn't wait. I couldn't even say why, but one thing I definitely knew I could not do was wait.

Disgusted, Mademoiselle MacKenzie handed me the wooden bathroom pass, and I beat it out of there before she could say "*Au revoir.*"

But I didn't head for the bathroom. Instead, I went downstairs—the language labs are on the third floor—to the guidance office. I wasn't even sure why I was heading in that direction until I saw them. The doors to the guidance office, and across from it, the teachers' lounge.

That's when I knew. Claire. Claire, touching my shoulder, just before fifth period. She had wanted to tell me something, but she hadn't gotten the chance. Her eyes—those pretty blue eyes—had widened as she'd looked down at me, and filled—I knew it now, though at the time, I think I had been too worried about myself, and my stupid chair position, to notice—with fear.

Fear. *Fear.*

I burst into the guidance office and startled Helen, the secretary, half out of her wits.

"I need to know what class Claire Lippman's in," I said, throwing my books down onto her desk. "And I need to know *now.*"

Helen stared up at me, her expression friendly but quizzical. "Jess," she said. "You know I can't just give you confidential student—"

"I need to know *now!*" I yelled.

The door to Mr. Goodhart's office opened. To my surprise, not just Mr. Goodhart, but also Special Agent Johnson, stepped out into the waiting area.

"Jessica?" Mr. Goodhart looked perplexed. "What are you doing here? What's wrong?"

Helen had hit the button on her computer keyboard that made Minesweeper, which she'd been playing, disappear. Now she was bringing up the student schedules. Mr. Goodhart noticed and went, "Helen, what are you doing?"

"She needs to know where Claire Lippman is," Helen said. "I'm just looking it up for her."

Mr. Goodhart looked more perplexed than ever. "You know you can't tell her that, Helen," he said. "That's confidential."

"Why do you need to know where this girl is, Jessica?" Special Agent Johnson asked. "Has something happened to her?"

"I don't know," I said. Which was the truth. I didn't know. Except . . .

Except that I did.

"I just need to know," I said. "Okay? She said she had something to tell me, but then she didn't get a chance to, because—"

"Claire Lippman," Helen said, "has PE seventh period."

"Helen!" Mr. Goodhart was genuinely shocked. "What's the matter with you?"

"Thanks," I said, gathering up my books and giving the secretary a grateful smile. "Thanks a lot."

I was almost out the door when Helen called, "Except that she isn't there, Jess. . . ."

I froze.

And then slowly spun around.

"What do you mean, she isn't there?" I asked carefully.

Helen was studying her computer screen with

a concerned expression. "I mean she isn't there," she said. "According to this afternoon's attendance rosters, Claire hasn't been in class since . . . fourth period."

"But that's impossible," I said. Suddenly I felt funny all over. Really. Like someone had shot me full of Novocain. My lips were numb. So were my arms, holding onto my books. "I saw her just before fifth."

"No," Helen said, reaching for some printouts. "It's right here. Claire Lippman has skipped fifth through seventh."

"Claire Lippman has never skipped a class in her life," Mr. Goodhart—who would know, being her guidance counselor—declared.

"Well," Helen said, "she has today."

I must have looked like I was going to pass out or something, because suddenly, Special Agent Johnson was at my side, holding onto my elbow, going, "Jess? Jessica? Are you all right?"

"No, I'm not all right," I said. "And neither is Claire Lippman."

CHAPTER

16

It was my fault, of course.

What had happened to Claire, I mean.

I should have listened. I should have taken her by the arm and dragged her someplace quiet and listened to what she had to tell me.

Because whatever it had been, I was convinced, was directly linked to the fact that she was missing now.

"It's a beautiful day out," Mr. Goodhart said. "Maybe she just took off. I mean, you know how she likes to sunbathe, and with this Indian summer we've been having, attendance, especially in the afternoon, has been sliding. . . ."

I was sitting on one of the orange vinyl couches, my books in my lap, my arms limp at my side. I looked up at Mr. Goodhart and said, my voice sounding as tired as I felt, "Claire didn't skip class. They got her."

Special Agent Johnson had called Jill, and now the two of them were sitting across from me, staring, like I was some new breed of criminal they had only read about in text books at FBI training school or something.

"Who got her, Jessica?" Special Agent Smith asked, gently.

"They did." I couldn't believe she didn't know. How could she not know? "The same ones who got Amber. And Heather. And the restaurant."

"And who *are* they, Jessica?" Special Agent Smith leaned forward. She was looking like her old self again, her bob curling just right, her suit neatly pressed. Today she had on the diamond studs. "Do you know, Jess? Do you know who they are?"

I looked at them. I was so tired. Really. And not just from hardly having gotten any sleep the past couple days. I was tired *inside*, bone-tired. Tired of being afraid. Tired of not knowing. Just tired.

"No, of course I don't know who *they* are," I said. "Do you? Do you have any idea at all?"

Special Agent Smith and Special Agent Johnson exchanged glances. I saw him shake his head, just a little. But then Jill said, "Allan. We have to tell her."

I was too tired to ask what she meant. I didn't care. I truly didn't. Claire Lippman, I was convinced, was lying dead somewhere, and it was all my fault. What was my brother Mike going to say when he found out? He'd been in love with Claire for as long as I could remember. Granted, he'd never uttered a word to her in his life, that I knew of, but he loved her just the same. That year she'd starred in *Hello, Dolly,* he'd gone to every single performance, even the kiddie matinee. He'd gone around humming the title song for weeks afterward.

And I hadn't even been able to protect her for him. The love of my brother's life.

"Jessica," Special Agent Smith said. "Listen to me a minute. Amber. Amber Mackey, you know, the dead girl?"

I looked at her. There was enough energy left in me—not a lot, but enough—to go, very sarcastically, "I know who Amber Mackey is, Jill. She only sat in front of me every day for *six years.*"

"Agent Smith," Special Agent Johnson said in a sharp voice. "That information is confidential and not for—"

"She was pregnant," Special Agent Smith said. She said it fast and she said it to me. "Amber Mackey was seven weeks pregnant when she was killed, Jess. The coroner just completed his autopsy, and I thought—"

I blinked at her, once. Then twice. Then I said, *"Pregnant?"*

Mr. Goodhart, who'd been leaning against Helen's desk, watching us, went, *"Pregnant?"*

Even Helen went, *"Pregnant? Amber Mackey?"*

"Please," Special Agent Johnson said. You could tell he was way annoyed. "This is not something we want spread around. The victim's family hasn't even been told. I would ask that you keep this information to yourself for the time being. It will, of course, get out, as these things invariably do. But until then—"

But I wasn't listening to him anymore. All I could think was: *Amber. Pregnant. Amber. Pregnant. Amber. Pregnant.*

Which meant only one thing, of course. That Mark Leskowski was the father. The father of Amber's baby. He had to be. Amber would never have slept with anybody else. I mean, I was surprised she'd slept with *him.* She just hadn't been that type of girl, you know.

But I guess I'd been wrong. I guess she *had* been that type of girl.

But I'll tell you what type of girl she wasn't: The type to get rid of an unwanted pregnancy. Not Amber. How many bake sales had she organized to raise funds for the single moms of the county? How many car washes had she held to help out the March of Dimes? How many times had she passed me a Unicef carton and asked for my spare change?

Suddenly, I wasn't feeling tired anymore. It was like energy was pouring through me . . . almost like I was filled with electricity again, like I'd been that day I'd been struck by lightning.

Okay, well, not quite like that. But I was no longer exhausted.

And I'll tell you something else: I wasn't scared.

Not anymore.

Because I had remembered one more thing. And that was that the fear I'd seen in Claire Lippman's eyes? Yeah, that hadn't been there when she'd first started speaking to me. No, the fear hadn't shown up until later. Not until Mark Leskowski—*Mark Leskowski*—had strolled out of the guidance office and said hello to us.

Mark Leskowski. The father of Amber's baby.

Mark Leskowski, who'd sat at Table Seven— the make-out table—at Mastriani's and told me, when I'd asked him what he was going to do if his plans of making it to the NFL didn't work out, *"Failure is not an option."*

And your sixteen-year-old girlfriend giving birth to your baby, out of wedlock, the same year you were being scouted by colleges? That, to Mark, would certainly fall under the category of "unacceptable."

I stood up. My books fell to the floor.

But I was still holding onto Claire's sweater. It had never left my fingers, all afternoon.

"Jessica?" Jill climbed to her feet as well. "What is it? What's wrong?"

When I didn't answer her, Special Agent Johnson said, in a commanding voice, "Jessica. Jessica, do you hear me? Answer Special Agent Smith, please. She asked you a question. Do you want me to call your parents, young lady?"

But it didn't matter. What they were saying, I mean. It didn't matter that Helen, the secretary, was looking up my home number, or that Mr.

Goodhart was waving his hand in front of my face, yelling my name.

Oh, don't get me wrong. It was *annoying*. I mean, I was trying to concentrate, and all these people were hopping around me like Mexican jumping beans or whatever.

But it didn't matter. It didn't really matter what they said or did, because I had Claire Lippman's sweater. Her pink cashmere sweater that her mother, I now knew—though there was no rational way I *could* know this—had given to her for her sixteenth birthday. The sweater smelled like *Happy*, the perfume Claire always wears. Her grandmother gave her a new bottle every Christmas. People complimented her on her perfume all the time. They didn't know it was just *Happy*, from Clinique. They thought it was something exotic, something super expensive. Even Mark Leskowski, who sat in front of Claire in homeroom every day—Leskowski, Lippman—had said something about it once. Asked her what it was called. He'd wanted to buy a bottle, he'd said, for his girlfriend.

His girlfriend Amber. Whom he'd killed.

Just like he was going to kill Claire.

Suddenly, I couldn't breathe. I couldn't breathe because it was so hot. It was hot, and something was covering my mouth and nose. I was suffocating. I couldn't get out. Let me out. Let me out. *Let me out.*

Something hard hit me in the face. I started, and then found myself blinking into Mr.

Goodhart's face. Special Agents Johnson and Smith had him by both arms.

"I told you," Allan was yelling, "not to hit her!"

"What was I supposed to do?" Mr. Goodhart demanded. "She was having a fit!"

"It wasn't a fit." Jill looked really mad. "It was a vision. Jessica? Jessica, are you all right?"

I stared at the three of them. My cheek tingled where Mr. Goodhart had slapped it. He hadn't hit me very hard.

"I've got to go," I said to them, and, clutching Claire's sweater, I left the office.

They followed me, of course. It wasn't easy, though, because no sooner had I stalked out into the hallway than the bell rang. The last bell of the day. Kids poured out of the classrooms and into the corridors, slamming their locker doors, high-fiving one another, making plans to meet up at the quarries later. The halls were teeming with people, crowded with bodies, everyone streaming toward the exits.

And I let them take me. I let the tide sweep me away, through the doors and out toward the flagpole, where the buses were waiting to take people home. Everyone but the kids who'd come in their own cars or who had to stay after for ball practice or tutoring or detention.

Everyone but Claire. Claire wouldn't be making her bus today.

"Jessica," I heard someone yell behind me. Special Agent Johnson.

Somebody was waiting by the flag pole.

Somebody familiar. He was easy to make out in the hordes streaming toward the buses, because he was a head taller than most of them and was standing still, besides.

Rob. It was Rob.

A part of me was glad to see him. Another part of me didn't notice him at all.

"Jess," he said when he saw me. "Oh, my God. I heard what happened last night. Are you okay?"

"I'm fine," I said. I didn't slow down. I walked right past him.

Rob, falling into step beside me, went, "Mastriani, what's the matter with you? Where are you going?"

"There's something I have to do," I said. I was walking fast, so fast that I was pretty sure I had lost Special Agents Johnson and Smith somewhere back in the crowd in front of the buses.

"What do you have to do?" Rob wanted to know. "Mastriani, why are we *here?*"

Here was the football field, off to one side of the student parking lot. It was under the metal bleachers surrounding the field that Ruth and I had ducked, that day last spring when we'd been caught in the storm. The storm that had changed everything.

It didn't look much different, the football field, than it had that day, except that now it was in use. Coach Albright was standing in the middle of it with a whistle in his mouth, as his players streamed out from the locker room for practice.

Most of the cheerleaders were already there. They were holding auditions for Amber's position. It was sad and all, but what were they supposed to do? They couldn't do a pyramid with just nine girls. They needed a tenth. The bleachers were crowded with girls eager to take Amber's spot. When they saw Rob and me, they stopped chatting amongst themselves and stared. Maybe they thought I was there to try out. I don't know.

"Jess," Rob said. "What is the matter with you? You're acting really weird. Weirder than usual, even."

Coach Albright noticed us and blew his whistle. "Mastriani," he yelled. He knew me only too well from my many altercations with his more fractious players. "What are you doing here? Are you here for the tryouts?"

I didn't answer him. I was scanning the field, looking for one person and one person only.

"If you ain't here for the tryouts," Coach Albright yelled, "get off the field. I don't need you around, making my boys nervous."

I saw him, finally. He was just coming out from the gym, his shoulder pads making him look bigger than he actually was . . . though of course, he was pretty big without them. The bright sun shone down on his bare head as he hurried, helmet in hand, toward the rest of the team.

I headed toward him, meeting him halfway.

"Jess," he said, in some surprise, looking from

me to Rob, who stood just behind me, then back again. "What's up?"

I held out my hand. The hand that wasn't clutching Claire's sweater. I held out my hand and said, "Give them to me."

Mark looked down at me, a half smile on his face. He was playing it cool.

"What are you talking about?" he asked.

"You know," I said. "You know good and well."

"What's going on here?" Coach Albright demanded, stomping over to us. He was followed by most of the rest of the team—Todd Mintz, Jeff Day—and more than a few of the cheerleaders. It wasn't every day a civilian walked out onto the field and interrupted practice.

Especially one who wasn't even part of their crowd.

"Mark, this girl giving you a hard time?" Coach Albright asked.

"No, Coach," Mark said. He was still smiling. "She's cool. Jess, what's going on?"

"You know what's going on," I said, in a voice that didn't sound like mine. It was harder than my voice had ever been. Harder and, in a way, sadder, at the same time. "You all know." I looked around at the other ball players. "Every last one of you knows."

Todd, blinking in the strong sunlight, went, "I don't know."

"Shut up, Mintz," Jeff Day said.

Coach Albright looked from me to Mark and then back again. Then he went, "Look, I don't know what this is about, but if you got a problem with one of my players, Mastriani, you bring it to me during office hours. You do not interrupt practice—"

I stepped forward and sank my fist into Mark Leskowski's gut.

"Now give me," I said, as he dropped to his knees with a gasp, "your car keys."

Everything happened at once after that. Mark, recovering with amazing quickness, lunged at me, only to find himself in a headlock, courtesy of Rob. I was yanked off my feet by Jeff Day, who planned, I think, on hurling me over the nearest goalpost. He was stopped by Todd Mintz, who grabbed him by the Adam's apple and squeezed.

And Coach Albright, in the middle of the fray, blew and blew on his whistle.

There was a jingle, and something bright fell from Mark's waistband into the grass. Rob snatched it up and said, "Mastriani." By that time, Jeff, unable to breathe with Todd crushing his larynx, had dropped me. I reached up and caught the keys on the fly, one-handed.

And then I turned around and started for the student parking lot.

"You can't do this," I heard Mark bleating behind me. "This is illegal. Illegal search and seizure. That's what this is."

"Consider yourself," Rob said, "under citizen's arrest."

They were following me. They were all following me, Rob and Mark and Todd and Jeff, Coach Albright, and the cheerleaders. Like the Pied Piper of Hamlin, leading the village children to their doom, I led the Ernest Pyle High School football team and pep squad to Mark Leskowski's BMW, which was parked, I saw when I got to it, just a little bit away from Ruth's Cabriolet and Skip's Trans Am.

"Oh, my God," Ruth said, when she saw me. "There you are. I've been looking all over for you. What's . . ."

Her voice trailed off as she got a look at what was behind me.

"This is *bullshit*," Mark bellowed.

"Mastriani," Coach Albright yelled. "You put those keys down. . . ."

Only I didn't listen to him, of course. I walked right up to Mark's car and put the key in the lock to the trunk.

Which was when Mark tried to make a break for it. Only Rob wouldn't let him. He reached out almost casually and grabbed hold of the back of Mark's shirt.

"Let me go," Mark screamed. "Lemme freaking go!"

Only he didn't say "freaking."

I turned the key, and the BMW's trunk popped open.

And that's how Special Agents Johnson and Smith found us, a minute or so later. With the entire in crowd of Ernest Pyle High School crowded around Mark Leskowski's BMW, while Rob Wilkins hung onto Mark, and Todd Mintz hung onto Jeff Day (who'd also tried to get away at the last minute).

And me half-in, half-out of Mark Leskowski's trunk, trying to get Claire Lippman to start breathing again.

CHAPTER

20

"Well, that certainly sucked," Claire said, later that evening.

"Tell me about it," I said.

"No, I mean, really. Like, I was sure I was going to die."

"You *looked* dead," Ruth pointed out.

"Really?" Claire seemed very interested in this piece of information. "How, exactly, did I look?"

Ruth, sitting on the windowsill across from Claire Lippman's hospital bed, glanced at me, as if unsure whether or not to answer the question.

"No, really," Claire said. "I want to know. So in case I ever have to do a death scene, I'll know how to look."

"Well," Ruth said, hesitantly. "You were really pale, and your eyes were closed, and you weren't breathing. But that was on account of the tape over your mouth."

"And the heat," Skip pointed out. "Don't forget the heat."

"It was a hundred and ten inside that trunk," Claire said cheerfully. "That's what the EMTs said, anyway. I would have died of dehydration way before Mark got around to killing me."

"Uh," Ruth said. "Yeah. About that. That's the part I'm not real clear on. *Why* did Mark want to kill you, again?"

Claire rolled her pretty blue eyes. "Duh," she said. "Because he saw me talking to Jess."

Ruth looked over at me, where I was sitting between the dozens of huge floral arrangements people had been sending to Claire ever since she'd been admitted. She was due to be released in the morning, so long as the results of her CAT scan confirmed she had not, in fact, suffered a concussion. But still the flowers kept coming.

Claire Lippman was actually a lot more popular than I had ever realized.

"Explanation, please," Ruth said.

"It's really very simple," I said. "Amber Mackey got pregnant—"

"Pregnant!" Ruth cried.

"Pregnant!" her twin brother echoed.

"Pregnant," I said. "And she told Mark she wanted to keep the baby. In fact, Amber wanted him to marry her, so they could raise their child together, be a little happy family. That's what they were talking about that day at the quarry, when Claire said she saw Amber and Mark keep going off together, alone. Amber's pregnancy."

"Right," Claire said. "Only a pregnant girl-friend was not part of Mark's plan for the future."

"Far from it," I said. "Getting married, or even paying child support, was going to totally mess up Mark's football career. It was, in his book, 'unac-ceptable.' So, near as we can figure it out—and he hasn't confessed, mind you—Mark beat Amber up, in the hopes that she'd change her mind, and left her somewhere—probably in his trunk. They're checking it for fibers now. When that didn't man-age to convince Amber to see things his way, he killed her and tossed her body into the quarry."

"Okay," Ruth said. "I can see all that, I guess. But what about Heather? Wasn't Mark with you when Heather disappeared?"

"Yes," I said. "He was. That was the point of Heather's attack. Mark was starting to feel the heat, you know, with the Feds breathing down his neck, so he figured if another girl got attacked at a time during which he had a rock-solid alibi, he'd be in the clear."

"And what's more rock-solid," Skip said, "than the fact that he was with the FBI's friend, Lightning Girl."

"Right," I said. "Well, more or less. And you know, it worked. When Heather disappeared, no one suspected Mark."

"Except you," Claire pointed out.

"Well," I said, a little guiltily. "I didn't exactly suspect Mark." Quite the opposite, in fact. I'd been convinced no one as hot as he was could be a criminal. Stupid me. "But that house . . . I knew there was something up with that house. So when I started asking around about it, Mark got scared again and had Jeff Day—the same guy who'd kidnapped, and then later beat up, Heather—make some threatening phone calls. And then, when that didn't seem to be working, Mark and Jeff broke into Mastriani's, poured gasoline all over the place, then lit a match and burned the place down."

At least according to Jeff Day, who'd started crying like a baby the minute the cops arrived, then spilled his guts like a squashed caterpillar.

"Mark's biggest mistake," I went on, "was enlisting the help of someone like Jeff Day in getting him out of his little jam. I mean, on the one hand, it makes sense, since Jeff is used to taking direction from Mark, on account of Mark being the team quarterback and all. But Jeff needs a *lot* of direction. He was always coming up to Mark and asking him what to do . . . especially right before the first class of the day, homeroom."

"Where Mark sat in front of me," Claire said. She was taking her role as victim very seriously, and waved her arm, the one with the IV in it, as much as possible, to bring attention to her infirmity. "So of course this morning, when he and Jeff were whispering before the bell rang, something about the way they looked . . . so sneaky . . . triggered something. I just knew. I can't say how I knew. I just put two and two together. But you can't go to the police, you know, with a hunch. But I figured I could go to Jess—"

"But when she tried," I said, "Mark caught her. And she was so startled—"

"I ran," Claire said gravely. "Like a startled fawn."

I wasn't so sure about the fawn part. Claire was kind of tall for a fawn. A gazelle, maybe.

"But Mark went around the side of the building," I said, "and caught up with her, and—"

"—hit me right back here," Claire said, touching the back of her head, "with something heavy. And when I woke up again, I was in his trunk."

"My guess is he was going to take her to the house on the pit road," I said, "and do to her what he'd done to Amber. . . ."

"So what," Ruth asked, "is going to happen? To Mark, I mean?"

"Well," I said. "With the help of Jeff's testimony—which I'm sure he'll give in exchange for a reduced sentence for his part in the whole thing—Mark's going to prison. For a long time."

Which was really going to mess up his plan for getting drafted right out of college by the NFL.

Before anyone could say anything in reply to this, Claire's parents, Dr. and Mrs. Lippman, came back into the room.

"Oh, thanks, kids," Mrs. Lippman said, "for keeping our baby entertained while we were gone. Here, Claire, a mint-chocolate-chip shake, just like you asked."

Claire immediately lost all of the animation she'd had when talking to Ruth and Skip and me. Instead, she fell back against the pillows, and let her head loll a little.

She was really milking this for all she was worth. Well, she was in the drama club, after all.

"Thanks, Mom," she said weakly.

"Well, uh," I said. "We better go."

"Yeah," Ruth said, slipping off the windowsill. "Visiting hours are up anyway. Bye, Claire. Bye, Dr. and Mrs. Lippman."

"Bye, kids," Dr. Lippman said.

But Mrs. Lippman couldn't let it go with a simple good-bye. No, she had to come over and give me a big hug and call me her little girl's savior and tell me that if there was anything— anything at all—she or her husband could do for me, I needed only to ask. The Lippmans—along with, surprise, surprise, Heather's parents— were starting a Restore Mastriani's Fund. I wished that instead they were starting a Pay Off Karen Sue Hankey's Medical Bills Fund, so that Mrs. Hankey would drop her suit against me.

But beggars can't be choosers, I guess, so all I said, as Mrs. Lippman attempted to squeeze the life out of me, was, "Uh, you're welcome."

Barely escaping with my ribs intact, I followed Ruth and Skip out into the hall.

"Whew," Ruth said. "Now I know where Claire gets her sense of the dramatic."

"Tell me about it," I said, scrubbing Mrs. Lippman's lipstick off my cheek, where she'd kissed me.

"Should we stop by and see Heather?" Skip asked as we made our way to the elevators.

"They released her already," I said. "Broken

arm, couple of busted ribs, and a concussion, but otherwise, she's going to be all right."

"Physically," Ruth said, punching the button marked DOWN. "Mentally, though? After having been through what she went through?"

"Heather's pretty tough," I said. The elevator came, and we all got on it. "She'll be back out there, shaking her pompons, in no time."

"Yeah, but what is she going to shake those pompons for?" Ruth wanted to know. "I mean, without Mark and Jeff, the Cougars don't have much of a chance of making it to State. Or anywhere, for that matter."

"Well," I said. "There's always the basketball team. None of them, as far as I know, have murdered anyone lately."

"So, Jess," Skip said, as the doors opened to the hospital lobby. "How does it feel to be a hero? Again?"

"I don't know," I said. "Not so great, really. I mean, if I'd have been able to figure it out sooner, I might have saved Amber. Not to mention Mastriani's."

"How *did* you figure it out?" Ruth asked. "I mean, how'd you know Claire was locked inside Mark's trunk?"

It was a question I knew I'd get asked eventually, though I'd been hoping against hope to avoid it. How was I going to explain that for a moment, I'd *been* Claire, inside that trunk? And all because she'd dropped her sweater . . . a sweater I'd just returned to her, by the way.

"I don't know," I lied. "I just . . . I just knew is all."

Ruth looked at me sarcastically. "Yeah," she said. "Right. Just like this summer, with Shane and the pillow. I get it."

Ruth got it, all right. I just hoped nobody else did.

"What pillow?" Skip wanted to know.

"Never mind," I said. "Listen, you guys, I better get home. My mom's having a big enough cow as it is, what with the restaurant, and now Douglas and this job thing. Not to mention Karen Sue's lawsuit—"

"I can't believe she's really suing," Skip said, looking indignant. "I mean, after Jess pretty much single-handedly caught a murderer and all, in her own school."

"Well," I said, a little sheepishly. "I did almost break Karen Sue's nose. Not that she didn't deserve it."

Ruth tactfully changed the subject.

"So what's with that, anyway?" Ruth asked. "Douglas, I mean. Comix Underground is totally skeevy. Why would anyone want to work there? It's always packed with members of the turtle patrol."

"Hey," Skip said, sounding offended. Skip, I knew, often shopped at Comix Underground.

"I don't know," I said with a shrug. "He's Douglas. He's always marched to a different drummer."

"I'll say." Ruth shook her head. "God, I'm sure glad I'm not living in your house. It's going to be like World War—" She broke off, and, looking toward the sliding doors by the ambulance bay, said, "Well, I was going to say World War Three, but I think I'm going to have to amend that to World War Four."

I followed her gaze. "What? What are you talking about?"

Skip saw him before I did. "Whoa," he said. "Alert the Pentagon. The Mastriani household has just gone to Def Con One."

And then I saw him. And froze in my tracks.

"*Mike!*" I couldn't believe it. "What are you doing here?"

Mike had obviously just come from the airport. He had an overnight bag with him and looked, to put it mildly, like crap. He hurried up to us and said, "How is she? Is she all right?"

"Why are you here?" I demanded. "Didn't Mom and Dad just drop you off at Harvard last *week*? What are you doing back?"

Michael glared down at me. "You think I could stay there, knowing what happened?"

"Mike," I said. "For God's sake. The insurance is going to pay to rebuild the place. It is not that big a deal. I mean, yeah, it's sad and all, but when I talked to Dad a little while ago, he was totally into the idea of redesigning, He is going to kill you when he finds out you—"

"I don't care about the stupid restaurant," Mike said, his voice filled with scorn. "I didn't come back for that. It's Claire I care about."

I blinked at him. "Claire?"

"Yes, Claire." Mike looked down at me worriedly. "Claire Lippman. How is she? Is she going to be all right?"

I could only stare up at him with, I am sorry to say, my mouth hanging open. *Claire?* He'd come all the way back from college—probably blown an entire semester's allowance buying an airline ticket at the last minute—because of *Claire,* a girl who'd never spoken to him before in her life? Were *both* my brothers insane?

It was Ruth who said, "Claire's going to be fine, Michael." I was proud of her for being so calm. Ruth had had her own little crush on Mike awhile back. Her summer romance with Scott had apparently cured her of it, however. "She's just, you know, being held overnight for observation."

"I want to see her," Mike said. "What room is she in?"

"Four-seventeen," Skip said, at the same time that I finally burst out with, "Are you crazy? You flew a thousand miles just to make sure a girl who doesn't even know you're alive is okay?"

Mike looked down at me and shook his head, completely unimpressed by my outburst. "Tell Mom and Dad," he said, "that I'll be home in a little while."

Then he started for the hospital elevators with a little swagger in his step, as if he were Clint Eastwood or somebody.

"Visiting hours are over," I yelled after him.

But it didn't do any good. He was like a man

possessed. He disappeared into an elevator, his shoulders thrown back and his head held high.

"That," Ruth said, gazing after him, "is the most romantic thing I have ever seen."

"Are you kidding?" I was appalled. "It's completely . . . well, it's . . . it's . . ."

"Romantic," Ruth finished for me.

"Sick," I corrected her.

"I don't know," Skip said. "Claire's kind of hot."

Ruth and I looked at him. Then we both looked away in disgust.

"Well," Skip said, "she is."

Ruth took me by the arm and started steering me from the hospital. "Come on," she said. "We'll stop at the Thirty-one Flavors on the way home, and you can pick up a pint of Rocky Road for your mom. That'll help, you know, when you break the news about Mikey."

We walked out into the mild evening air. The sun had only just set, and the sky to the west was all purple and red. It occurred to me that Mark was probably looking at the same sky. Only he'd be looking at it from behind bars—from now on.

Talk about unacceptable.

"First thing we'll do tomorrow," Ruth was saying as we started for her car, "is reschedule your chair audition—"

I groaned. I had forgotten all about Mr. Vine and my after-school appointment with him.

"Then," Ruth said, "you're going to have to get Rosemary to send you some photos of kids who've got some reward money posted for their return. You're going to need some extra cash, what with the restaurant and Karen Sue's lawsuit and all."

I groaned louder.

"And then, I'm sorry, but we're going to have to do something about your hair. I've been thinking about this, and I really believe what you need are some highlights. Saturday nights they do free coloring at the beauty college—"

"Hey," Skip said. "Saturday night Jess and I are going to the movies."

"Oh, you are not," Ruth said grumpily. "I can't have my brother dating my best friend. It's too gross."

Skip looked taken aback. "But—"

"Shut up, Skip," Ruth said. "It's gross, and you know it. Besides, she doesn't like you. She likes that guy over there."

Curious what she meant, I looked where Ruth was pointing. . . .

And saw Rob, leaning against his bike, waiting for somebody.

And that somebody, I knew, was me.

He straightened up when he saw me and waved.

"Oh," I said. "Uh, I'll see you guys later, okay?"

"Whatever," Ruth said airily. "Come on, Skip."

"But—" Skip was looking at Rob with suspicion and, it must be admitted, a small amount of dismay.

"Sorry, Skip," I said, patting him on the arm as Ruth led him away. "But Ruth's right, you know.

It'd never work. I can't stand all that hobbit stuff."

Then, giving Skip a big smile to show how sorry I was, I hurried over to where Rob was standing.

"Hey," I said, my smile turning shy.

"Hey," Rob said. His smile wasn't shy at all. "How are you doing?"

"Oh," I said with a shrug. "Okay, I guess."

"How about Claire?"

His mentioning Claire reminded me of Mike. I couldn't help scowling a little as I said, "Oh, she's going to be fine."

Rob didn't seem to notice the scowl. "Thanks to you," he said.

"And you," I said. "I mean, you kept Mark from getting away."

"That was nothing," Rob said modestly. "Anyway, I stopped by to see if you wanted a ride home. Do you?"

"You bet," I said. "Hey, did your mom tell you about my dad's scheme to keep all the staff from Mastriani's on payroll while the new restaurant's being built? He's converting Joe Junior's from counter service to waitress-only service."

"She told me," Rob said with a grin. "Your dad's a good guy. Oh, hey, here, I almost forgot."

He turned from the side compartment, where he'd been fishing out his spare helmet for me, and dropped something heavy into my hand. I looked down and was shocked to see that I was holding his watch.

"But," I said, "this is your watch."

"Yeah," Rob said, "I know it's my watch. I thought you wanted it."

"But what are you going to use?" I wanted to know. Although I have to admit that, while I was asking this, I was already strapping the thing on.

"I don't know," Rob said. "I'll make do." When he turned to hand me the helmet and saw that his watch was already on my wrist, he shook his head. "You really *are* weird," he said. "Do you know that?"

"Yes," I said, and stood up on my tiptoes to kiss him. . . .

Only before I got a chance to, somebody nearby cleared his throat and said, "Uh, Miss Mastriani?"

I turned my head. And stared.

Because there, standing in front of a black four-door sedan—clearly an unmarked law-enforcement vehicle—stood a tall man I had never seen before. The man, who was wearing a hat and a trench coat even though it was like seventy degrees outside, said, "Miss Mastriani, I am Cyrus Krantz, director of Special Operations with the Federal Bureau of Investigation. I happen to be Special Agent Johnson and Smith's immediate supervisor."

I glanced at the car behind him. It had tinted windows, so I couldn't tell if anyone else was inside of it.

"Yeah," I said. "So?"

Which probably sounded pretty rude and all, but I had way better things to do than hang around outside the county hospital talking to the FBI.

"So," Cyrus Krantz said, seemingly unmoved by my rudeness, "I'd like a word with you."

"Everything I've got to say," I told him, pulling Rob's spare helmet over my head, "I already told Jill and Allan." I swung a leg over Rob's bike and settled in behind him. "Ask them about it. They'll tell you."

"I have asked *Special Agents* Johnson and Smith about it," Cyrus Krantz replied, enunciating their proper titles, which I had neglected to use, with care. "I found their answers to my questions unsatisfactory, which is why I've had them removed from your case, Miss Mastriani. You will now be dealing with me, and me alone. So—"

I lifted up the visor to my helmet and stared at him in shock. "You *what?*"

"I've removed them from your case," Cyrus Krantz repeated. "Their handling of you has, in my opinion, been amateurish and entirely unfocused. What is clearly needed in your case, Miss Mastriani, is not kid gloves, but an iron fist."

I could only stare. "You fired Allan and Jill?"

"I removed them from your case." Cyrus Krantz, director of Special Operations, turned around and opened the rear passenger door of the car behind him. "Now, get into this car, Miss Mastriani, so that you can be taken to our regional headquarters for questioning about your involvement in the Mark Leskowski case."

I tightened my grip around Rob's waist. My mouth had gone dry.

"Am I under arrest?" I managed to croak.

"No," Cyrus Krantz said. "But you are a

material witness in possession of vital—"

"Good," I said, snapping my helmet's visor back into place. "Go, Rob."

Rob did as I asked. We left Cyrus Krantz in our dust.

The only problem, of course, is that I'm pretty sure he knows where I live.